W9-BYK-631

ℋhat the critics are saying...

ℬ

Make Her Dreams Come True

"This was one of the most amazing erotic stories I've ever read. I've read so many that, most of the time, they all blend together as just another erotic story. This is the first that's truly touched my heart. Each touch, each movement, each turn of control has a specific purpose, all leading to the beautiful and touching conclusion of this story. I highly recommend this story, even for those who don't usually enjoy erotic romance." ~ *In the Library Reviews*

"Hill's talented prose and descriptions bring scenes to vivid life. After reading this provocative and sensual story, I'll never look at a trip to the mall in the same way!" ~ *Romantic Times*

"Joey W. Hill weaves her magic through words, seducing your mind just as Daniel seduces Meg with his words. Beautifully written, MAKE HER DREAMS COME TRUE is true romantic erotica. I do not recommend this book for the gentle reader, but instead recommend it very highly for those who are open to the mind and heart of this talented writer." ~ *Romance Reviews Today*

Holding the Cards
2004 Eppie Award Winner

"Joey W. Hill has written an incredible story for readers of passion—a feast of delights sure to tease, please and appease!" ~ *Romantic Times*

IF
WISHES
WERE
HORSES

JOEY W. HILL

ELLORA'S CAVE
ROMANTICA® PUBLISHING

An Ellora's Cave Romantica Publication

www.ellorascave.com

If Wishes Were Horses

ISBN 9781419950612
ALL RIGHTS RESERVED.
If Wishes Were Horses Copyright © 2004 Joey W. Hill
Cover art by Syneca.

This book printed in the U.S.A. by Jasmine–Jade Enterprises, LLC.

Trade paperback Publication December 2004

Also by Joey W. Hill

ॐ

Enchained (*anthology*)
Forgotten Wishes
Make Her Dreams Come True
Nature of Desire 1: Holding the Cards
Nature of Desire 2: Natural Law
Snow Angel
Virtual Reality

About the Author

ॐ

I've always had an aversion to reading, watching or hearing interviews of favorite actors, authors, musicians, etc. because so often the real person doesn't measure up to the beauty of the art they produce. Their politics or religion are distasteful, or they're shallow and self-absorbed, a vacuous mophead without a lick of sense. From then on, though I may appreciate their craft or art, it has somehow been tarnished. Therefore, whenever I'm asked to provide personal information about myself for readers, a ball of anxiety forms in my stomach as I think: "Okay, the next couple of paragraphs can change forever the way someone views my stories." Why on earth does a reader want to know about me? It's the story that's important.

So here it is. I've been given more blessings in my life than any one person has a right to have. Despite that, I'm a Type A, borderline obsessive-compulsive paranoiac who worries I will never live up to expectations. I've got more phobias than anyone (including myself) has patience to read about. I can't stand talking on the phone, I dread social commitments, and the idea of living in monastic solitude with my husband and animals, books and writing is as close an idea to paradise as I can imagine. I love chocolate, but with that deeply ingrained, irrational female belief that weight equals worth, I manage to keep it down to a minor addiction. I adore good movies. I'm told I work too much. Every day is spent trying to get through the never ending "to do" list to snatch a few minutes to write.

This is because, despite all these mediocre and typical qualities, for some miraculous reason, these wonderful characters well up out of my soul with stories to tell. When I manage to find enough time to write, sufficient enough that the precious "stillness" required rises up and calms all the competing voices in my head, I can step into their lives, hear what they are saying, what they're feeling, and put it down on paper. It's a magic beyond description, akin to truly believing my husband loves me, winning the trust of an animal who has known only fear or apathy, making a true connection with someone, or knowing for certain I've given a reader a moment of magic through those written words. It's a magic that reassures me there is Someone, far wiser than myself, who knows the permanent path to that garden of stillness, where there is only love, acceptance and a pen waiting for hours and hours of uninterrupted, blissful use.

If only I could finish that darned "to do" list.

I welcome feedback from readers—actually, I thrive on it like a vampire, whether it's good or bad. So feel free to visit me through my website www.storywitch.com anytime.

Tell Us What You Think

We appreciate hearing reader opinions about our books. You can email us at Comments@EllorasCave.com.

IF WISHES WERE HORSES

ও

Chapter 1

ℰℴ

She had been in a small town too long if she could excuse trespassing with the lame excuse of "no one will mind". Particularly since she, the chief of the Lilesville police department, was the one doing the trespassing.

Something about the forty-two acres of undeveloped land backed up against her own five-acre property called to her, however, and had done so since she had moved in almost six weeks ago. The adjacent property belonged to Justin Herne, a local resident who operated a sex shop in the small town's unincorporated area. Her cop's mind rationalized that he'd want to stay on the good side of the law, even if he did discover her there.

She winced at the thought. She hadn't met the man, but she was sure he'd get that derisive sneer to his lip that all those who walked the shades of gray between law and lawlessness did when they caught a police officer bending the rules. *You're no better than me, sister.*

Still, it wasn't as if it hadn't been done by the previous occupants of the house. A well-worn path led into the woods from her back stoop and tonight she'd finally given in to the urge to follow it, to find solitude.

The parallel to the changes she had made in her life over the past several months did not escape her.

Her divorce had been painful and predictable. Overworked big city detective, too many hours on the job, irascible and closed off when she was at home. When she found the lipstick on his collar and put it together, he claimed she drove him to the other women. She shot four holes into their bedroom wall over his head, went out, got drunk and humped an accommodating salesman hanging around the bar of a nearby hotel. In the morning she woke with sour breath, a massive headache, and a broken heart.

Sarah moved from her fast warm-up walk into a jog, stretching out her thigh muscles, but she couldn't outrun her thoughts.

God, divorce sucked. It wouldn't be so bad if it were possible to have the memories surgically removed as part of the process, but every other second she remembered. Small images as lethal as a sliver of glass gently drawn across a major artery. His cheek against hers as they danced at their wedding. His warmth curled around her in bed. The bed that waited cold and empty for her now.

He'd turn her over and start a gentle suckling of her breasts as she lay there, half between sleep and dreams. His hand would slide down her stomach, slip under the waistband of her pajama bottoms and press against her, a slight movement of two fingers against her clit, his other fingers delving deeper into her moistening, willing folds as she turned her mouth to his, awake now and rising to the passion in his kiss.

Truth be told, the sex had become not-that-great except in those half-dream, half-awake times, but early in the marriage it had been good. Maybe it was that way for everyone. She didn't know when it had gotten to be something she had to will herself to do, like an exercise workout. Something she knew would make her feel better after she did it, but getting started and in the zone took effort.

She thought her husband was a wonderful lover in the beginning, but as time went on there was something desperate to his performance, like a man trying to hold onto something he thought was running away from him.

But I was right there. Wasn't I?

She turned off the path and scrambled up a wall of dirt and vines, her major muscle groups screaming as she pushed herself, her blood roaring in her ears. She got to the top, picked up another path and tried to push herself back into the same hard run. Her lungs rebelled, forcing her to a shuffling trot. A moment later she gave up and just stood, hands on knees, head low, wheezing for oxygen, trying to establish a rhythm to her erratic breathing.

She found a rhythm, but it was not her own. Sarah realized she was matching the cadence of her lungs with a beat that was not coming from her pulse.

She straightened, forcing her breath to an even keel so she could listen. A drum. About six seconds between beats.

This was private land. She should not be here, and she should definitely not be following her curiosity through the woods, pinpointing the location as she moved silently.

Perhaps it was the cop instinct suggesting that people did not go deep into the woods in the middle of the night to beat a drum for innocuous reasons. Or perhaps it was something else drawing her. As she got closer to the sound, the pace of the beat stepped up and she felt her blood stir with it. There was a hush in the forest as if all the creatures of the night had stopped to listen. The heat that prickled over her skin did not come from the leaping shadows that heralded a fire somewhere just ahead.

Now she heard voices, raised in a chanting song that reminded her of the ceremonies she had attended as a child with her Cherokee grandmother. The voices were devout, strong, aligned with the drums. Men's and women's voices.

Either someone else was trespassing on Herne's property, or he had given them permission to be there. Either way, it would do no harm to take a look in case something came up. And whether it was something or not, she *would* talk to Mr. Herne this week and get his permission to run on his land.

Her guilt somewhat assuaged, Sarah moved forward. She saw the flickering of the fire but not the fire itself, and as she got closer to the noise she realized it was because the chanters were below her in a ravine. She went to her belly and inched forward so she could peer over the lip.

Nine were gathered around the bonfire. Seven circled the fire, including the drummer. Two were inside the circle, closer to the flames. The light plumbed the depths of the ravine, starkly outlining the movements of man or beast, or both.

Since Sarah was part Cherokee, there was something vaguely familiar about what she was seeing. Nevertheless, her cop side wished for the comfort of her sidearm.

One of the two in the circle was a man. She knew that because from the neck down he was naked, save for the paintings of symbols on his chest, arms and thighs. He was also impressively aroused, his cock rising from a dark tangle of hair like the shadows of the ravine. Okay, the guy was more than impressively aroused. He was hung like a much larger mammal. In fact, it was the size of his erection that made her think he might be closely related to the animal whose head he was wearing, a ten-point stag whose eyes glittered brown and feral in the firelight. A pair of straps, crossed over his broad chest and back and buckled under the cut of the deer's pelt, anchored the noble skull to the man's, but even with the help of the straps, his shoulders and neck had to be strong to take the weight.

He sprang up from a kneeling position and turned with the beat of the drum, offering, displaying…yes, he was displaying himself, to the woman across the fire from him.

She was naked as well and heavy-breasted, with generous hips and symbols painted on her body. A crescent crystal hung from a plain cord around her neck. She wore no headdress as he did, and Sarah saw the woman with dark, shoulder-length hair and bright green eyes was probably in her early thirties. Her hands were outstretched and crusted with mud as she sang the chant with the others. She cupped her breasts and spun in lithe invitation.

A woman in the circle began to sing alone, the others dropping to a soft murmuring chant behind her. Her voice was a soft rush of sound, like wind moving through marsh grass.

The woman is the altar.
The center of the circle.
Death and life spiral around her.

Inside the circle, the naked woman's arms folded across her chest, her focus inward and yet intent upon the man.

Sarah gasped as the deer-man leaped the tall bonfire. No running start, no warning, just from a crouch to a soaring burst of power in a moment. It was not the effeminate elegance of a ballet move. No, he exploded over the flames like a primal warrior, muscles bunched at thighs and back, neck corded and taut.

He landed at the woman's feet in another crouch, his pale body curled toward the earth in a posture of deep obeisance, his fingers tented against the ground, their tips sunk into the soft earth. His haunches tightened and released with the beat of the drum, a rippling, infinitesimal rhythm of buttocks and back thigh muscles that suggested the erotic movements of copulation.

As the woman looked at him, a smile lit her features and brightened the ravine with a power greater than the heat of the fire. The hair rose on Sarah's damp neck.

Something was there, part of the woman, linking them all, even Sarah, for the energy flowed through the stillness that gripped the ravine. It did not feel threatening as much as it simply swept over and overwhelmed the senses. Sarah felt it through the stuff of her sweat suit, the heat above her, the press of earth below, against her breasts, her loins, her thighs.

The crouched man pressed his jaw against the side of the woman's calf, careful not to harm her with the antlers. He had his hand on her leg, holding her. She touched his bare shoulder and swayed, still softly singing the chant along with the others, her eyes vividly alive and yet far away at once.

He kissed her feet, her knees, the flesh just above her pubic mound. He did it in a formal, fervent way as she raised her hands out and above herself again, her nipples tightening in want even as she sang praises to those they were worshipping. Now a man from the circle sang out, in a deep baritone that resonated through the air.

Lord of life
Death and the underworld.
Sun to the Goddess's moon.
Male to Female.
Strong in the physical world
as She is in the spiritual.

Magic springs from their Joining
Balance is in their unity
Matter and spirit brought together
Death to Life and Life to Death.

Something new comes from something ending.
A new beginning.
The cycle continues.

The deer-man rose to one knee, and the priestess kept her arms spread out to either side of her. He kissed each breast, a reverent brush of lips over the top of each curve that Sarah felt on her own flesh. It was sexual, but it was more than that. Her reaction trembled deep inside her, begging to be immersed in this moment of strong connection between two bodies, between the people and the Beings they were revering, between all the polarities in the world. It was a yearning for belonging so strong she felt it not just in the imagined touch of lips on her breasts, but in every vulnerable energy point inside her body.

When the deer-man stood, he was taller than the priestess, even discounting the headdress. He took her hands and the drummer's tempo increased, the chants of the circle becoming more insistent, building until the ground vibrated.

Two of the circle stepped forward, and Sarah saw they were all unclothed. Each took a gentle hold of one arm of the priestess and lowered her to the earth. The antlered man stood over her, firelight dancing across his skin, etching the shadows of his tense shoulders, his upright cock, the intent set of his jaw. The two assistants returned to their places, and the priestess lifted her arms and opened her legs, inviting him into her body.

> *He is worthy*
> *Lord of the Sun*
> *Consort to the Moon*
> *His Seed placed in the fertile Earth*
> *brings nourishment to us all.*
>
> *Birth, growth and death*
> *All begin again in Their joining.*
>
> *As above, so below*
> *As above, so below*
> *As above, so below*

The chant and the drums matched the pounding of her heart, the rushing of her blood, the heat of her loins. Sarah watched, mesmerized as the man knelt between his lady's legs and slowly laid himself upon her, holding his upper body with the strength of his arms. His hips pushed her thighs wider and she undulated, a sensuous movement taking him into her willing womb. Sarah heard the priestess's soft moan, his masculine grunt, and her own moist entrance contracted, weeping with the desire for total fulfillment.

The priestess caressed his face with her hand as she raised her arms and laid them over her head, opening herself to him fully. His knees dug into the earth as he increased the power of his strokes, his flanks quivering with each penetration, his head dropping to rest just over hers so their eyes were locked, though his were shadowed by the mask, his shoulder muscles corded to take the increase in forward weight.

> *The Lord and Lady become one*
> *As we are all One*
> *To renew our spirits*
> *Our Earth*
> *Ourselves.*

> *This joining is the transformation we know*
> *This is the moment we transcend who we have been,*
> *but we do not forget the path we have traveled.*
> *We grow above it, along the spiral*
> *So below becomes above*
> *then below again*
> *And life never ends because death never ends.*

The strong voice of the soloist singing carried above the increased power being placed on the drum and the stamping of the circle, which now matched the rhythm of his thrusts. Sarah's own hips pressed into the earth in time with the priestess's, her thighs loose as if she too were open to this joining. Her fingers clenched the earth and she realized when salt touched her lips she was crying. As the fire illuminated each face, she saw most in the circle were weeping.

She did not know when she had shifted from a cop's suspicion to immersion in a ritual she knew nothing about, but understood like an instinctive response to a mother's touch. She did not think of herself as a spy any longer. She simply was a part of what was going on below her.

A harsh moan tore from the man's lips and he threw his antlered head back, keeping his thrusts in even measure with the furious pounding of the drum. The woman beneath him exposed her lovely throat, her heavy breasts wobbling back against her sternum as she lifted her hips higher to match his power, taking him deeper, her face eclipsed by delight, an ecstasy as much spiritual as physical.

Spots of light clouded Sarah's vision. Staring too long at the two etched by the roaring flames might have caused them, or her own light-headed state, but the flashes were there, and a wave of heat roared over her. She gasped at the beauty of the lights that obscured the bodies of the participants, as if they had burned away all but the purest essence of every person.

A moment later, or it could have been an hour, Sarah became aware of the crackle of the fire, the return of cricket and frog song. A light breeze touched her face and moved the trees above her. The antlered man and the priestess were gone.

Sarah raised her head, blinked and studied the clearing below. The drummer beat out a soothing cadence, like a mother's recorded heartbeat for a baby's lullaby. The other six sat in their circle around the fire, passing around a goblet filled with liquid and tearing chunks off of a round of bread.

Had she actually blacked out? Or had the two inside the circle been there at all?

Oh, Sarah. Get a grip.

She couldn't deny the Indian part of her blood was thrumming on high alert. It knew that just because she couldn't explain something, it didn't mean it had not been there, a real part of an existence beyond human understanding. Cops liked intuition, trusted it. Her partner in Chicago had told her several times he thought her spiritual roots gave her an edge she was too willing to discount. He claimed they were there in ways she didn't even notice because they were so much a part of her.

In this case, those roots were so shell-shocked she hadn't noticed the disappearance of two wild naked people, one with a stag head's strapped to his skull.

Okay, Sarah. Enough trespassing and eavesdropping for one night. She slithered back down the incline, made it to shaking legs, and staggered for home with a full and confused mind.

Chapter 2

ॐ

Despite that, she slept better than she had in a long time, as if her inadvertent participation in the ritual had cleared some crap out of her worry closet and given her a night off. She didn't wake until nearly two in the morning, surprised to find her hand drifting to touch herself, her mind absorbed with thoughts of the antlered man. Soaring over those flames, the woman opening to him, his buttocks tightening with each thrust into her. In her drowsy state, Sarah imagined herself beneath his body, her thighs open to him, her arms around his slick and powerful shoulders.

She rested her fingers on her clitoris over her underwear. She twitched just a bit, and the nerve endings stirred. It had been so long since she'd done this. God, he'd been so...male. Just pure male. Muscle, sweat, cock, testosterone, broad shoulders, tight ass. She had noticed everything, because a cop did, but she felt like she could describe it all in perfect detail. From the curved lines of his collarbone to the way his muscles slid smoothly over his ribs as he turned, the flex of his thighs as he crouched, the way his heavy testicles hung at the base of his cock as it jutted up attentively. The tilt of his head, the glitter of his eyes, while he watched the woman he would worship.

That was what had been so moving, so mesmerizing. He had revered and possessed her at once.

Sarah let out a soft whisper of breath, almost a moan as her legs quivered and opened wider, inviting one of her hands under the band of her panties.

Yes. Her body sighed in relief. *Girl, we've needed this. Where have you been?*

She knew the answer, but before she could frantically stave it off, it was in her head. Her ex-husband's cruel comment that she had become a dead fish in bed, not just in her enthusiasm, but in the rasping dryness of her pussy to his advances.

Asshole. Asshole. Asshole. She pressed her fingers harder against herself, the way she might press them against her eyes to hold back tears, but the moment was lost. Her desire had fled.

A floorboard squeaked.

Sarah rolled, pulled her nine millimeter and its holster from the nightstand. She had the gun in her hand and her butt on the floor, her back against the mattress, before her mind had disengaged from the previous thought. As a result, she wasn't sure if her mental reaction—*Shit*—applied to her aborted attempt to rouse herself or the fact she had an intruder. Both possibilities seriously irritated her.

Silence settled over the house, but whether it was that sense her partner had referenced or something else, she knew the intruder was still there. Lilesville had very little violent crime, so it was likely she had a burglar who didn't realize she was at home. She tended to jog from home to the station, the five-mile morning and evening run keeping her in condition, and she kept her squad car at the station.

She leaned over, peering around the corner of the mattress. Whoever it was, he wasn't in her bedroom yet. Taking herself to a crouch then straightening, she padded to the door on silent feet, the gun held pointed upward in a two-hand grip, her finger on the trigger guard.

She could have called out to scare off whoever it was, but if he was light-fingering her house, he was hitting others as well, and she wanted to catch the bastard rather than giving him the chance to run.

She moved into the hallway, glanced into the one-room guest bath, and eased up to the corner that led into the living room, listening for a telltale rustle or breathing that would indicate someone was waiting on the other side. Nothing.

She stepped squarely into the doorway, the gun steady and pointed straight at a man.

He sat in her wingback chair, his profile slightly toward her, the opposite side of his face bathed in moonlight from the window so his features were outlined in silver, but the part facing her was in shadow. He had his legs crossed, one hand on the chair arm, the other resting with casual elegance on his leg, both hands where she could see them.

He was as still as a woodland creature. His eyes, deep set, dark and large, shone through the darkness of her living room.

"If you get out of that chair, I'll shoot you. I'm a police officer."

"I know that. It's why you can see my hands, Chief Wylde."

Deep, cultured and smooth, all the right syllables soft and rich like the first bite of chocolate cake. Sarah did not lower the gun. "This is breaking and entering, asshole."

"I broke nothing," he said. "You left your back porch door unlocked. You've gotten too used to country living. It's safe here." His head cocked and she saw a dark eye glitter, almost black. "But not that safe."

"Trespassing is still an option," she snapped.

"Wouldn't that be the pot calling the kettle black?" His teeth showed in what she supposed he called a smile. "That was my land you were on tonight, and you invaded the privacy of a sacred religious ceremony. Hardly the law-abiding thing to do, wouldn't you say?"

Sarah stepped forward, returning the gun to a point-up position, though not relaxing her guard. The change in position put her where she could see his countenance fully. Moonlight glinted off his skin as it would off marble. Her cat purred on a cushion behind him in the window seat, unconcerned that she could have been massacred in her bed.

Justin Herne had an elegant body that suggested a runner's health regimen rather than a weight lifter's. He had strength, she felt it, but his face bordered on gaunt, giving it a pale sharpness and hunger. The hunger unsettled Sarah, and made her think of what she had been doing right before he came into her house. At least, she hoped it was before he came into her house and had been able to hear her rustlings and soft moans. Otherwise, she *would* shoot him.

She couldn't get a good sense of his eyes, so she snapped on the light switch, which turned on the dim buffet lamp by the nearby couch.

He did have dark eyes, the rich tone of mahogany. When he smiled that feral smile as he did now, it made them more focused, like a faceted gem placed under light, made more hypnotic and overwhelming by its brilliance.

Many handsome men embellished their countenance by choosing a hairstyle that framed their face. Few men had the sculptured features that Justin Herne had so that they could pull the hair back into a queue, showing shining wings of chestnut brown hair molded against a finely shaped skull. His eyebrows were perfect curves, from his high brow to the bridge of his straight nose.

Men with rugged faces had always appealed to her. She preferred a Harrison Ford to a Brad Pitt. Justin Herne was neither pretty nor rugged. Like the statue of a Roman god, his smooth alabaster muscles and features were perfectly defined, all extraneous material chiseled away. The hint of gauntness gave his artistic perfection a haunting, human touch.

He stood up, and her gun came back down. He was taller than she was, more physically powerful. In her profession, she was used to that, and knew that her training evened the odds. But there was a power working here that had nothing to do with whether or not he could beat her in an arm wrestling match. Nothing she had learned in police training had prepared her for it.

She had no comfort zone with men who were sexually confident. As a cop, she knew how to fence words with criminals whose filthy attempts to get a rise out of her fell short. The riding and suggestive comments of other cops were also part of the rough world she had to face. Perversely, the stares of a group of shirtless construction workers or a good-looking cable guy's smile made her fumble.

Justin Herne emanated the sexual confidence of a god, so strong it seemed to come at her from all directions, even though all he'd done was rise from the chair.

Her nose betrayed her, stealing her judgment. Beneath the clean chambray shirt that lay in soft folds against the planes of his body and the well-tailored black slacks, she smelled the earth, the residue of perspiration dried on his skin after coitus, the faint aroma of an animal's hair. Her cop senses confirmed what her woman's senses told her. The man facing her was the antlered man.

"I guess it makes sense, the guy owning the property being the star of his own show," she said caustically. "So can you tell me what you were doing tonight? Or do I need to know the secret handshake?"

She wanted to turn on a brighter set of lights to dispel this mood, the sense of intimate isolation with him, but she couldn't risk the distraction.

"You can search on the Internet for the mechanics of Wiccan ritual, including the Great Rite, officer." He moved forward, and though he did it slowly, Sarah still felt the threat of him. Not of physical peril, but of something more fragile, as if the ground beneath her were becoming unstable as he pulled matter to him, giving her nowhere to run. He was annihilating her boundaries with his intent eyes and physical presence.

"There was nothing mechanical about what I saw," she said, her voice harsh. "You need to stop right there. Now." Was that panic in her voice?

"No, there wasn't." He stopped, and she realized with professional horror that he was standing with his chest against the barrel of her gun. "The Great Rite is an expression of one of the deepest mysteries. There are no words to adequately describe it. It brings opposites together to create balance."

She was sliding down a cliff and there was no one to offer her a rope. "Is that your best pick-up line?" she scoffed. She was all too aware her arms were trembling.

"No, this is." He snagged the wrist of her gun hand and yanked her arm and the weapon to the outside of her hip. At the same moment he closed his grip on her other hand and jerked it down to his erection. She found herself cupping his balls in her shaking fingers, his hard length against her palm through the fabric of his slacks. The pulse of his large organ throbbed under the sensitive skin of her wrist.

She could fight him. She could twist away, inflict pain on him to effect a retreat for both of them, but she didn't. Sarah stood rigid, staring up at him, wishing for something she couldn't name. He destroyed her intention to resist by staying still, holding her close to him, the lift and fall of his chest no more than a deep breath's distance away from the rapid trembling of hers.

He studied her face for a long moment. He released her gun hand to reach up and trace the line of her cheek, shielding her eye from the moon's light coming in through the window. His finger moved forward, under the soft skin of her eye, down the side of her nose, etching the curve of one nostril, then rested on her parted lips. He dipped his touch within, just the slight movement needed to find the moisture between teeth and gum and spread it on the fullness of her bottom lip.

He kept his other hand firmly on hers against his cock, not allowing movement, just making her experience the pulse of that rigid organ against her damp palm.

"Is the safety on?" he asked, his voice a breath of sound against her face.

Somehow a brain cell survived to send a message to her fingers so that she shifted her grip, clicked it back on. Damn. She should have thought to check the safety before he had. But he had thought to protect them. Protect her. It did nothing to ease the growing fire in places in her body a total stranger should not be igniting.

She nodded, and he twisted her hand, a strong but not painful force. The weapon dropped several inches to the sofa. His arm went around her waist, his hand against her back, and the last space was closed, her breasts against his chest, her thighs against his. Her hand was free, for now his other was on her neck, tangling in her hair, pulling her head back. Her fingers curled into a claw against his hip.

"No," she said. "You've been…with another woman."

"You don't give a damn about that," he said, his eyes glowing in the dim light like a wolf's. "She is part of you, part of the same Goddess that claimed the Great Lord as her Consort through me, renewing the land and our spirits with our joining."

It was true in a deep, primitive way she did not understand, and it scared the hell out of her. She didn't want to be swept away like this.

He brought his mouth down on hers before she could say anything else, and God, she didn't know what she'd have said.

Something about this night and seeing the ritual had opened the wounds of her divorce, as well as that familiar and overwhelming yearning in her. He was here like an answer to that aching emptiness. Just…fuck it.

Fuck me, please. Make me forget. Make me believe again. Make it everything, so nothing else will matter.

"I will," he muttered, and she realized she had spoken aloud, though she did not know which part of the words had made it to her lips. Sarah held onto his hard biceps as he devoured her mouth, scraping his teeth against her soft lips, bearing her tongue down beneath his, stroking it even as he dominated it inside the wetness of her mouth. He made it lie pliant beneath his will and quiver there.

He was an intruder in her house. A stranger. She had just seen him participate in a ritual that would horrify the notion of moral conduct in civilized society. But every gasp for breath brought that animal smell to her, the sweat of the ritual beneath his clean shirt, the hunger in his body. Her body shoved away her inhibitions in a way it never had, mowed them over like an eager child overriding its mother's feeble protests in the face of an offer of candy. This wasn't just candy. This wasn't even a whole candy store. This was a child's paradise of endless treasure to discover, summer days that never ended, bare feet in the mud and all the mysteries of the universe expressed in ways so simple they did not have to be spoken.

She whimpered in the back of her throat when he shifted, pressing his cock against the dampening crotch of her plain cotton panties. He hoisted her, wrapping her legs around his waist, and her hair fell along his jawline as he lifted her above him. His hands cupped her ass cheeks and opened her to the tips of his fingers. It made her squirm in erotic shivers, which rubbed her against the heat of his cock, pressed hard against her clit with pinpoint accuracy.

She was dizzy. The walls were moving. No, she was moving. He was taking her down the hall to the bedroom. She felt like she was falling down a tunnel, like a slide where there was no stopping the momentum without getting her palms blistered. She held onto his shoulders and he bit her throat, using his tongue to soothe even as he bit down again, harder. His fingers were under her underwear, the tip of his middle finger probing her tight rear entry. Her legs spasmed, kicking the wall, reacting to the strange whirl of sensation the unfamiliar touch speared through her.

There was a scrape as they passed her dresser, and then something cold and metal touched her. Before Sarah registered the different sensory input, he had her down on her back on her bed and her arms above her head. Panic shot through her at the snap of the steel bracelets of her own handcuffs, their rattle against the wrought iron bars of the headboard. The sudden blast of fear shoved away the tide of lust.

"What the—Herne, you son of a—"

"Ssshhh."

The world had not stopped spinning from her trip down the hallway, and her panic enhanced the disorientation, keeping her from getting her bearings back in time. His palms clamped under her knees and he pushed her legs up into the air and back, so her body folded over and her kneecaps were shoved to meet her shoulders. He threaded her thrashing feet between the railings of the headboard, four slats apart so her legs were spread. He hooked them there so she was held by them and the strength of his hands against the back of her thighs. She stared helplessly up at him through the vee of her legs.

"You can't—"

He was on his knees before her vulnerable pussy and ass, and she had a glimpse of those dark eyes before his head bent and his hot, moist breath touched her cunt through the cotton. He sucked the fabric and her clit into his mouth, rubbing his tongue against them. The alternating friction of the three caused her body to shake erratically, the only thing she could do in this position. There was no straining possible, no arching, just the fixed point of her pussy and that convulsive little bounce that made his mouth a tiny staccato of pressure against her full to bursting tissues.

He growled, there was no other word for it, and hooked his finger in the panties. He tore them off her body, the seams scraping her skin with the roughness of the motion. His tongue stabbed into her pussy and she cried out, a prolonged sound between a wail and a moan that begged for whatever it was he could offer her. She was going to come, he was stroking her clit, making wet sucking noises of enjoyment that were driving her crazy, yes, now he was stroking harder, alternating light with rough, he was—nooo. He moved back into her pussy, taking away the driving force of the sensation, and when she bounced, the bump of his nose was all the relief she was given. No relief at all.

She gave a shocked cry as his middle finger, wet with her arousal, invaded her anus and fingered her there, setting off electric sparks of reaction she never knew existed. Her knees rubbed the sides of her breasts, and her nipples were begging for attention against the stretched thin fabric of her tank as she lay helplessly raised like a baby with her ass in the air.

"Tell me you want more, Sarah," he demanded, his mouth and fingers working her.

Don't. Don't.

"You bastard—"

He bit, just the barest pressure of his teeth closing on her clit. She rocked against his still finger in her ass and his tight canine hold on her pussy, whimpering. Waves rolled through her, but it was not enough. The surf roared in her ears, beckoning.

"I can do this all night, Sarah," he murmured, his lips playing on her pussy. "So ask for it, or I'll torture you, with pleasure."

"More," she whispered.

Still he did not move. She looked down between her splayed legs and he looked at her, holding her clit in his mouth, his tongue doing idle flicks, his eyes hot and steady on hers.

"More," she snarled. "More!"

He straightened, held her with one hand on her thighs and freed his belt. Sarah's eyes widened as he leaned over her, his body pressed between her legs. Before she could work her feet free of the railings to thwart his intent, he had reached through the opening of the slats and looped the belt around one ankle. He threaded the tongue through the rails and looped the other end around the other ankle and cinched it with a clever knot. Now her ankles were firmly tied and held to the railings, her knees posed over her head without him having to exert his weight against her.

"Herne." She yanked against the cuffs holding her wrists to the same headboard. Her voice trembled. She hated it, hated herself. "Don't."

He braced a hand on either side of her head and eased down between her trembling legs. His hips were against her upturned ass, his rigid cock against her weeping, bare pussy.

Furious tears filled her eyes. Not from a physical fear but an emotional one. He knew it, she could see he knew what she was feeling, as if her psyche were as laid open to him as all of her orifices. She wanted to hate him for it, was sure she would, but at this moment in the darkness there was just fear and desperate need. She saw images just behind her disintegrating shields, images of death and gunfire, her ex's closed and resentful expression. A message pounded in her head behind all of that, a truth she was too frightened to face.

She wasn't even sure what message she was trying to give him with her one word protest, but she thought Herne knew. It terrified her that he might know her heart and body at this moment better than she did.

"You asked for more, Sarah. I'm going to give you more." He nuzzled her ear, licked her neck. "But I won't stop. I'm going to fuck you so well you're going to lose consciousness. This will all be a dream. You won't be sure if you want to savor it or regret it. But you won't forget it. Not ever. I'm taking away that option." He hesitated, staring down into her face, and she sensed something there, something she did not understand. "The other two choices, to savor or regret, those will be yours."

He rose on his knees above her and unfastened his trousers. The thick, pale cock came free as he lowered the zipper, revealing he wore no underwear. Her mouth went dry. He took the trousers to his knees and that was all. He leaned forward, holding the weight of his cock in his hand, and eased the organ into her wet pussy. His eyes never left her desperate ones.

Her thighs shook, overcome by nerves and desires, and she made a strangled noise at his inexorable push forward. There was a moment of feminine fear, for he did not know her body, and she was helpless to prevent the pain of an incorrect approach or too-hard thrust, but his invasion, while relentless, was slow, an easing into her contours. By the time his heavy sac pressed warm and hairy against her ass, she thought he must be seated all the way to her womb.

She was gasping for breath, deep, shuddering draws. There was no tenderness to this. However, his sexual dominance was not being inflicted as a punishment. This was not sex without emotion, not mindless fucking. There was something strong and powerful here, like an act of religious fervor. No thought, just action and overwhelming blinding immersion. She didn't even know him, and yet she needed him to be in her body like this, needed his face this close to hers, close enough to kiss, but he didn't. Not now. She knew he wanted her watching him without any excuse other than cowardice to close her eyes.

He moved deeper, and then withdrew. She'd had at least one lover that knew to move slow, but not like this. Herne withdrew a millimeter at a time, pausing between each movement, his attention never leaving her face. He watched every quivering breath, the pull of her lips into her teeth, the half gasp, half whimper as he made his way slowly out of her, and his intensity of focus increased the power of her response.

"What are you doing?" she managed in a ragged whisper.

He stopped, the ridge of his broad head just inside her opening, and her body rocked, convulsed as she fought to grip him and keep him in. He pushed forward, that same slow glide, this time to refill her. It reminded her of the flow of molasses over the spout of a pitcher, so thick that even when it left the tip and gravity took over it did not hurry, sliding to the top of the pancake, making its way to the edge, filling in every crevice as it went.

Sarah cried out again, a long, low sound as his cock stroked its way up inside her. He brushed his lips against the corner of her eye and answered her question.

"Destroying you, Sarah. Creating you. Possessing you."

Each word, each phrase accompanied another small movement, making her strain for his words as frantically as for his penetration. His belt and the cuffs would have cut into her flesh if he had not kept his weight against the backs of her thighs, holding her helpless.

For the second time in one night, the salt of her tears touched her lips. She was crying, not from anger or fear but against the overwhelming sensual response of her own body which laid open her emotions and made them as unprotected as her pussy and ass to his stimulation and assault. He curled his arms around her head, sheltering her, giving her his musky scent and the press of his heated chest against her face. His lips touched the track of one tear a moment before he covered her.

He raised his hips while holding his upper body in that protective position. She screamed into his flesh as he pulled full out of her and then thrust back in. Molasses merged with fire into a blaze of consummation, burning so slowly that ecstasy almost became pain, but she was past the point of caring. Her whole being was shaking, and though she could not hold him, she let him hold her to keep her from shattering because there was no choice and no one else. He was what was holding her together in the darkness. At that moment, defying all logic or reality she was his, utterly.

"I could lose myself in you," he muttered.

She felt as if she was already lost, and his words took her deeper into the maze of her emotions.

"I want to make you wetter than you've ever been," he said, his voice caressing her senses. "I want to drive home tonight with my cock and balls drenched in you, Sarah. I want to feel your wetness dry on my skin."

The chambray fabric and hard buttons of his shirt rubbed against her bare skin, and somehow her nakedness against his state of almost full dress made her even more defenseless against him. Surely the ground beneath her was going to shatter as his thrusts rolled her hips back, pushed her down, again, and again.

"Justin..." His familiar name was on her lips like a rose he had pressed into her hand.

"Come for me, Sarah. Come deep and hard, let me feel your pussy grip me. I want to hear your soul scream."

How could she deny him with that hard cock driving into her like a pile driver slamming into the ocean floor, demanding the soft silken terra give way, yield to that invasion, make way for a permanent alteration in the contours?

She'd been too much of a wisecracking teenager to feel like a virgin when she lost her sexual innocence. *This* was losing her virginity, this disintegration of every wall, every defense, no anchor, totally vulnerable and catapulted into mind-blowing pleasure.

She shattered with a scream that vibrated off her windows and bedroom mirror and echoed into the forest behind her home. He held her, the hardness of his upper body against her breasts, his hips still plunging, his thigh muscles straining against the inside of hers, pale soft female flesh against firm male skin and coarse hair. The thump of his testicles against her ass was a thunderous slap jolting her body, driving it higher, driving the blood from her head and the oxygen from her lungs. Energy was being pulled from every part of her body to meet the force of an explosion that the human body seemed too frail to withstand.

She went over, not in a freefall or leap but in a starburst, her muscles shuddering, contracting desperately at the point of most charged contact, his cock in her pussy. The orgasm resonated through her and outward, sweeping her away into a place where she drowned in darkness and found stillness, the most peaceful of endings.

Chapter 3

ೲ

The pattering of rain. The stone cottage had a tin roof, painted a dark green to help it blend into the forest even more than it already did. One of the many things that had charmed her into purchasing the house was the rainstorm that had occurred the day she looked at it. She heard that soothing drumming and remembered she was part of something bigger than herself, rhythmic forces that renewed life everyday with their actions. A reminder that the same was possible for her.

Sarah opened her eyes and slowly focused. Some light filtered in through the fabric shades. The window was cracked, so she smelled the rain and the forest it cleansed. She didn't remember opening the window, but...

Her eyes focused on what lay beside her on the bed and she jerked straight up, her legs screaming in protest at the unanticipated movement. Her muscles ached from an activity they had not been accustomed to performing recently. Hell, even when she had been having regular sex, it hadn't been anything like last night.

The handcuffs lay on the bed. Threaded in the two bracelets were three of the white daisies that grew wild and abundant around her back door.

Sarah jumped as the phone blared next to her bed, as intrusive as a knife shoved in her gut. She hesitated, then snarled at herself. She was the police chief. Goddamn it. She was supposed to answer her phone. If it was him...

"Wylde."

"Chief, this is Leon. We've got a body in the woods."

Sarah swung her feet to the floor. "What?"

"Not in Lilesville," Leon said. "Just over the line in Marion. Chief Wassler called and asked if you'd come to the site and take a look."

"I'll be there. Where is it?"

"Not more than a couple miles from your place. Go up Highway 6 toward Marion, and a man will be at the street waiting to flag you. Do you need transport?"

"Rain's easing up and I've got my bike here. Have Dexter meet me at the site with a car."

"Okay. Damn, Chief. We haven't had a murder in these parts for a hundred years."

* * * * *

She had no time for a shower, though she desperately wanted one. She smelled him as she pulled on her jeans, that musk of male seed between the juncture of her thighs, mingling with her own erotic scent.

The job had never let her down, never confused her. She'd focus on that now and worry about the rest later. The body in the woods didn't give a damn about her love life. Sarah pulled on her black placket Lilesville police shirt, tucked it into the jeans, tugged the bill of her yellow and black police cap down and threaded her ponytail through the back. She secured her shoulder holster and was on the way to the crime scene in less than five minutes.

When she'd left Chicago, she could have gone in one of four compass directions to leave it behind. She had gone southeast. Lilesville was a town more than ninety minutes away from a town of any size, on the Gulf side of the Florida panhandle. It had that peculiar mishmash of graceful homes next to shacks crowded up around the waterfront and was surrounded by acres of protected wetlands and vibrant green marshes. It was not a town that produced murderers, only a mix of eccentric intelligentsia, old salts and redneck fishermen.

As Leon had said, an officer stood next to the rural highway, just over two miles from the turn off to her home. The uniform waved her down the service road behind him, his expression grim. She bumped along it for a half mile and found Chief Wassler waiting for her at the end of it.

Eric Wassler typified a small town chief of police. Fifties, heavy jowls, a bit of a paunch, and a kindly face with stern cop eyes. Sarah had been amused to find out from her men that his favorite pastime was dirt biking at the local open range areas. He'd served as an advisor to the hiring committee that had offered her the job in Lilesville.

During her first week, he had come by to introduce himself, and she liked him right off. He wasn't pretentious or territorial, showing no embarrassment when he told her he had been born and raised in the county, and had come back within five years of leaving the Academy. He had served in law enforcement here for nearly thirty years.

"Morning," he said, tipping his hat. "Appreciate you coming out."

She inclined her head. "Sorry for the circumstance."

He lifted a shoulder. "The rest of the way's on foot, Chief. Up that hill there."

She left the bike, fell in beside him as they headed into the woods, following a path marked by orange flagging tape. "Who found the body?"

"A kid, damn it. He was out here on his mountain bike with his dog."

 "No evidence of tire tracks, but we've had rain off and on the past several days. We think she was already here, maybe came here by herself or willingly with the perp." We found a backpack. Looks like it was hers. Had female stuff in it, change of clothes, that type of thing. In fact, it looked like she was living out of it, not just a day hiker."

"An extended camping trip?"

"Not exactly." Wassler shook his head. "Something's off. From what's in that pack, I'd think maybe she's a drifter."

"A woman drifter suggests an addict, or mentally unstable."

"That's what the crime scene suggests, also," he said. "Hell, Chief, that's one of the reasons I wanted you to see it. I don't have a lot of experience in this. My guys are mostly rookies or small town transfers. I had to get out the goddamn procedure manual this morning to go over the steps to secure a potential murder scene."

"One thing I always trust, Chief, is a good cop's gut."

Chief Wassler met her steady gaze, and his unshaven jaw relaxed a fraction. "She was doing some kind of weird ritual."

Sarah went cold. "What do you mean, ritual?"

"Best to have you take a look. Hard to describe. It gave me the creeps, I'll tell you that. You handle any ritual murders before?"

She shook her head. "You think you've seen it all, then someone else thinks something up."

"Guess so. For me, that's always meant all the ways kids can think of to vandalize school property, or the excuses people have for getting behind the wheel when they've guzzled one too many." Dead leaves rasped under their feet, decaying and nurturing the roots of the trees waving mint green new growth over their heads, filtering fresh sunlight onto their faces.

"Going to be a hell of a pretty day after that good rain. Damn." Wassler pulled out a change wallet, began to remove several quarters. He grimaced at Sarah's questioning look.

"My grandson and I have a bet. I'm supposed to give him a quarter each time I curse. He's supposed to give me one every time he does."

"So who's winning?"

"I think he's got his first year at Harvard pretty much in the bag."

Sarah found herself smiling. "How old is he?"

"Eleven. Mouth like a sailor, but since he's at the age he's doing it consciously to impress his friends, he can also shut it down. Harder when you've been doing it all your goddamn life." He stopped, pressed his lips together, rolled his eyes. Sarah fished out a quarter, put it in his hand.

"Here. For the college fund."

He shook his head, pocketed the change. "Once we give this to the press, I'm going to have to deal with a hundred million details. The mayor wants to have a public meeting to calm folks down. I was wondering if I could ask a second favor."

"So long as it's not looking at another dead body. I have a one per week rule."

She mentally cursed herself at his look. "My apologies, Chief. Homicide cops tend to develop a sick sense of humor to deal with this shit—I mean, this type of situation."

She had seen plenty of death serving as a detective in Chicago. She knew how to shut down her emotional side. She couldn't keep what she saw from seeping into the cracks of her soul and tarnishing it, but she'd learned to make a mostly impermeable shield with the jokes and an intent focus on getting the job done.

He grunted. "I know you're a good cop. I wouldn't have asked you here, otherwise. I read about that drug bust. I know you take the job seriously. You just took me off guard, is all."

Sarah pushed away the images that his words stirred on the charred battlefield of her memory. Her mind was fighting off enough disturbing images this morning. "Maybe you should call me Sarah."

He nodded. "Eric, then. Take a look down there."

They had topped the knoll. Sarah looked down.

It was a different ravine. However, there were enough similarities to what she had seen last night to make the hair rise on her arms.

A black substance marked the boundary of the circle, and nine flat stones had been placed along it at even intervals. A goblet of water, a candle, a branch of a live oak and a censer marked four points of the circle. A pentagram had been drawn in the cleared area with the same dark powder. The remains of a bonfire were evident inside the interior pentagram of the design, a ring of ashes and charred wood. A drum lay on its side inside the circle.

There were two key differences in the scene below. A dead cat, its throat slit, was placed next to the live oak branch. The dead woman was near the bonfire.

"Jesus," Sarah murmured. "Is that how you found her?"

Eric nodded. He stared above the crime scene, at the tops of the trees directly across from them. "I had my guys cordon off the area."

The naked body lay half in and out of the pentagon. The victim looked as if she had been in the process of having sex with someone. Her body was spread open, her neck arched back. Her knees and legs were drawn up, as if to absorb the thrusts of a lover. Her ankles rested in shallow dents pounded into the ground.

Sarah absorbed all this as she made her way down into the ravine. She took her time, placing each step carefully, logging the images each change of view brought to her. Death always made her angry, in or near her jurisdiction even more so. Death like this in a small, quiet place where it shouldn't happen offended her deeply, though she knew it could happen anywhere. She just hoped the man she had been with last night was not part of it. She focused, pushing away the thoughts, aware of Eric Wassler two paces behind her.

"I can see why you thought you might be dealing with a murder. Got a thought on the cause of death?"

"We won't know until the coroner gets here, but we're thinking exposure. She froze to death."

Sarah stopped, looked back at him. "You're joking."

"Do I look in a joking mood?" he snapped.

She let that pass. She'd nursed too many rookies through their first corpse not to recognize the signs of stress. "What makes you think she froze to death on a night when the temperature didn't fall below sixty?"

"Frost. She's got fucking frost on her."

She noted multiple cop-type shoe prints around the body, indicating the Marion force hadn't been as careful to follow procedure as they should have been, but they had done better than she would have expected.

Even though Wassler had warned her, the effect was startling. A frost-like substance rimmed the victim's blue lips and embossed the point of an angular shoulder, the tip of her bare breast, the insides of her thighs. Sarah touched the shoulder in one small spot, felt the cold. She brought the white powdery substance to her lips. Ice.

"Son of a bitch," she murmured. "This woman was a hard user." Sarah drew Eric's attention to the needle tracks on the arm. "I'm willing to bet the coroner will find the same on the backs of her knees."

The bumpy column of her sternum was visible between small breasts, which might have been larger if she had eaten occasionally, rather than living on whatever she had shot into her veins. Sarah knew the signs. This woman would have been an ER OD statistic waiting to happen.

She raised her gaze to the woman's face. Her emaciated, drawn countenance didn't match her glorious, healthy fall of brunette curls.

Sarah fished out her pen. She passed the covered tip over the woman's forehead near the hairline, and inserted it between the scalp and a tight netting.

"Good quality wig," she commented. "Expensive. Either it belonged to the perp, or she stole it. She wouldn't have wasted good drug money on something that cost this much."

"So you think it could have been an overdose instead of murder?"

"Maybe." Sarah pointed with the pen to the area between the woman's spread legs. "That looks like knee prints to me. She had company. Maybe he ran when she OD'd, or maybe he shot the poison into her deliberately. It's hard to say. Coroner's report will tell us a lot more. Do you have any occult activity around here, Chief?"

"Not really. There's a Wiccan coven in Lilesville, which you may already know about. Justin Herne's linked up with it. He carries a lot of new age stuff in that shop of his, and he hosts a festival on his property each year."

"Could Justin Herne be involved in this?" She made herself say it, though the words felt like jagged glass in her throat.

Eric's reaction was not what Sarah expected. The man looked shocked to his foundations. "Sarah, he's been part of our community for a few years. His family has been in Lilesville for three generations."

"The man runs a sex shop, Eric," she pointed out. "And while Wicca is a lovely faith in its pure form, it does attract its share of crazies."

"It's not a sex shop, Sarah, not like an adult store with glory holes in the bathrooms. Heck, my wife loves to go there."

Now it was her turn to be startled. He lifted a shoulder. "Justin came to town four years ago and moved in with his aunt. Beatrice Smartley, a good woman. He took care of her until she passed away, then opened his shop just outside the corporate line in one of the old two-story shingle farmhouses. He renovated the place, had it re-landscaped. I think he's going to open a bed and breakfast. Nope. Instead he opens his store. It's called 'For Her'. He starts with high-class lingerie like Victoria's Secret, only European hand-tailored stuff. Meditation candles, perfumed soaps, all those things women like. A few vibrators…" He cleared his throat, looked away. "Tucked away in the back. I think yeah, women will like this place, but it won't last, there's not enough of a market around here."

He shifted, his attention going pointedly to the body, like he thought perhaps they might move the conversation elsewhere, but Sarah stayed where she was. "So what happened?" she prodded.

"He starts holding events related to his inventory. He hosts lingerie parties for birthdays and bachelorette shindigs, brings in instructors to teach sensual massage for couples." A ghost of a smile crossed his face, as much as he could manage with the dead woman so close to them. "Then, he draws in our senior citizens with requests for their homemade herbal soaps and things like that to go with his aromatherapy perfumes and such. He asks them to make up some of their sweets, and now he has a little serve-yourself coffee area in his sunroom to give shoppers a place to relax. Donates all the proceeds from the refreshments to the local senior citizen center."

"So why is it classified as an adult business? Sounds more like a fancy lingerie store."

"Well, over time, he started bringing in more elaborate sex toys, role-playing costumes, adult books and videotapes, erotic artwork and photography. But not your typical Deep Throat cheesy stuff. Herne caters strictly to couples and women."

"I still think that would be a little over the top for the folks of Marion and Lilesville."

"Some of it is," Eric admitted. "But contrary to popular opinion, people in small towns aren't any more narrow-minded than people in the city. They just don't like someone shoving stuff in their face, making them change faster than it suits them. Herne seems to have a talent for getting people to look at things differently, while respecting the way things are.

By the time he added that stuff, he was pretty well integrated into the community around here, and there was barely a murmur of protest. I hear more concerns about the non-Christian new age stuff than the sexual aids, and even that's been low-level complaints."

"Sounds like he would have gotten more business if he set up in one of the bigger cities. Why'd he stay after his aunt died?"

"I've asked him that. He says he likes it here, and big cities are overrated. Doesn't matter anyway. Guy has set up a unique operation. We've got people who drive as far as from Miami to visit his place. It's almost a damn tourist attraction."

"Hmm." Sarah sat back on her heels, digested that. She'd be the first to admit that her radar this morning was shot to shit. Still, she wasn't going to ignore the tingling in her gut. Something didn't ring true.

"I'd like to bring him out here, let him see this," she decided. "Use him as an informal expert witness. He might be able to tell us what some of the things used to perform this ritual mean. I can also see how he reacts to the situation. He might not have had anything to do with this, but if he's involved in occult activity in the area, he may have an idea who our knee-print person is. Would you mind if I go get him, bring him out here to see what I get out of him before the coroner takes over?"

"Not as long as I'm here when you do," Wassler said. "But I'm telling you, I've read up on Wicca. You know, when they first started practicing in the area, just to make sure they were on the up and up. A lot of it sounds pretty crunchy granola, like a spiritual movement stranded in the sixties."

Sarah straightened and gave the chief a level look, not without sympathy. "I get that you know Herne and like him. But you asked me here for my experience, so I need to tell you that this kind of perp, if there is one, is more often than not someone who is part of the community. It's almost never the drifter or the guy with the biker tattoo and bad attitude. Murderers don't go around with a big 'M' on their chests."

"And here I thought they carried business cards. Murderers, Local Chapter 106," he said dryly.

"Damn unions are everywhere." She smiled. "You're learning the knack, Chief."

"Let's hope I don't have to get used to it." Eric frowned. "We're a small community, and a close one. Don't you think a tendency toward homicide would show up in other types of behavior, some kind of warning?"

"Not always. But I've met Herne recently, and the last thing I get from him is 'flower child'. How about you?"

Chief Wassler looked down at the body. An uncomfortable expression crossed his face, as if Sarah's question and the corpse were joining forces to rile his stomach. "No, I don't get that from him, either. But there's something about Herne. He's protective by nature, particularly toward women. If I had to say anything about him, I'd say he'd have made a good cop. Or a priest, odd as that sounds."

"Well, let's give him his chance to play cop. Let's bring him here and see what he says."

"I could dispatch a car."

"No, Dexter should be here with mine by now. I'd like to see his place, and I want to see his face when I tell him what we need from him."

Plus, they needed to clear the air between them. With the stench of death in her nostrils, accomplishing that was going to take an aircraft wind tunnel. "I'd like to see the backpack before I go."

She joined Eric outside the cordoned area around the body and waited for one of his men to bring it to him.

"So what was the other favor you needed?"

"Hunh?" He pulled his attention from the body.

"The second favour." She prodded gently, shifted so she was in his line of sight. "You asked me for two."

"Oh. Shit, yeah. Safety presentation at one of the county middle schools Friday, the usual ten to fifteen minutes on drugs. Would you mind?"

"Not a problem, if you can give my man a ride back to the station while I go see Herne."

"Done deal."

The uniform brought the backpack and Eric passed it to Sarah. She pawed through the contents and immediately found a small stash of cocaine inside a makeup compact that hadn't carried face enhancements in a long time. There was no billfold, nothing to ID the body. There was only one thing other than the clothes and the drugs.

"Look at this." Sarah withdrew the palm-sized book, the type that card shops sold in a basket next to the cash register. *"Best-Loved Poems."* She cracked it open and in the center was a photo, just slightly bigger than a postage stamp, of a newborn infant. The poem on the page was from 1 Corinthians 13, Paul's first letter to the Corinthians.

Love is not selfish…

Sarah turned her gaze from the passage that had been read at her wedding and focused on the picture.

"Looks like a hospital photo, the kind they take the day the baby's born and staple to the file," Eric observed. "Odd. It's the only thing really personal in the pack."

"Not so odd. An addict will trade everything for the next hit. This wouldn't have had value to anyone but her."

Sarah sat back on her heels. They all started as infants, as fresh and unmade as the photo in her hand, but for some it ended the way it had for the woman behind her. The ache in her gut intensified, the telltale burn of her ulcer. It was a signal, a part of her intuition, and she didn't welcome it. The woman in the circle had not overdosed. She and Eric Wassler had a murder case. She'd bet on it.

Chapter 4

ಎ

Sarah didn't avoid what scared her or pissed her off. Herne had done both and she was going to confront him, on several different levels. He'd picked the wrong day to have himself associated with a murder.

Even so, she made herself roll Wassler's words over in her mind because she didn't know how much her distrust and animosity toward Herne had to do with what had happened last night. He'd thrown off her instincts. Damn him. Why did the man have to be potentially connected to a murder? It was as though he were determined to make her crazy.

She had imagined Herne's store as the typical aged brick or clapboard storefront commercial structure, with no windows and an asphalt parking lot and cheesy sign as the sum total of the store's exterior embellishment.

Though Wassler had prepared her for something a bit different, she was surprised to turn down a drive shaded with large water oaks hung with Spanish moss. A solid wood sign painted silver gray with a white border marked the entranceway off the rural highway. The carved rose in a deep red hue underscored the sandblasted navy blue lettering of *"For Her"*.

The house was attractively landscaped with beds of spring tulips and lush weeping cherry trees around the gravel parking area. They framed the old rambling farmhouse with its wide porches and white columns. Candlelight glowed behind jewel-toned stained glass in the front first level windows. Bright green acres of marsh stretched out behind the property, and Sarah watched a heron take flight out of the tall grasses.

She pulled into a parking space. As she got out and walked toward the front door, she passed a side courtyard which could be accessed from the parking area through a trellis of wisteria. It was cobbled in stone, and had a wishing pond and a fountain as the centerpiece. The water poured over a bronze sculpture of a long-haired mermaid and a winged man, an angel. They clasped one another in an intimate embrace. One of the angel's wings was wrapped around the mermaid's bare back, his other hand cupping her breast. Her fingers tangled in his shoulder-length hair.

The courtyard was enclosed in the trappings of an English garden. There were a couple of discreetly placed benches, purple phlox tumbling over artfully placed piles of smooth large rocks, white lilies coming up from the cracks. The branches of an old live oak formed a shaded canopy over the back of the courtyard.

He had wanted to create a mood before his clients ever crossed the threshold of his store, and Sarah felt it as much as saw it. She turned to look back the way she'd come, and saw how carefully he had transitioned from the reality of the highway. The atmosphere gently pried open the senses to other possibilities, other adventures.

That surprised her again, but it paled next to her shock when one of Lilesville's well-respected octogenarians stepped out onto the porch. Mrs. Jenkins carried a warm smile and a brown bag with an artful arrangement of straw poking out the top. The handles of the bag were tied with a ribbon and a fresh gardenia bloom to screen the contents.

She came through a door propped open with a gargoyle statue bearing a big grin and a penis so long Sarah thought it was a tripping hazard. Along with the statue, there was a cluster of spring flowers in a tin bucket and a bird feeder, a Goddess figure offering the winged creatures sustenance out of her generous lap, just under her pendulous breasts.

Mrs. Jenkins neatly avoided the statue's overendowed genitalia in her sturdy black heels.

"Hello, Chief Sarah," she said. "It's good to see you this morning. Doing some shopping?"

"A…a gift for a friend," Sarah said, deciding she didn't want anyone to know she was here on police business. The murder would be TV and radio news by dinnertime, and she didn't want speculation to run rampant.

Mrs. Jenkins nodded, a twinkle in her eyes. "You come by my house sometime soon and I'll hem that dress you wore to church last Sunday. It's coming down in the back. You young women have such busy careers, you don't have time to attend to these things anymore." She pressed Sarah's hand with a bony hand covered in soft flesh and went on down the steps, humming to herself.

Sarah watched her go, mildly mortified that Mrs. Jenkins had the impression the police chief was shopping for sex toys or lingerie for herself and too embarrassed to admit it. The lady who did alterations to supplement her Social Security check carried her gloves and wore her hat as if she'd planned to stop at a church meeting. Her delicate blue-veined legs rose above her shiny black shoes. The hem of her blue dress was trim and neat.

Would she ever be a Mrs. Jenkins, face lined and content, her soul quietly wise and accepting of past mistakes? Weariness settled on Sarah's shoulders. The stress of what had happened with Herne and another murder to solve weighed her down. She straightened her spine, chastising herself for the moment of weakness, and turned on her heel.

Justin Herne was framed in the doorway.

In daylight, she had expected him to be different, the spell broken, just a handsome man who by some trick of moonlight and a primitive ritual had worked magic on her senses.

Her heart caught in her throat. He *was* different in daylight. He was more magnetic, because the reality of him was more immediate and stark, those harsh, pale planes of his face, straight nose and thin lips more potent in their full detail.

He wore a black, close fitting T-shirt tucked into fitted black slacks. A small silver pendant of a stag's head fused to a pentagon hung on a slender silver chain around his neck. His dark hair was swept off his forehead and tied back as it had been before, but it did not give him the veneer of civility such a style should have suggested.

The short sleeves of his shirt revealed what she had felt last night. There was little softness to him, his muscles corded and lean, giving his body a tensile appearance. Strangely that made her heart hurt, as if she could stroke those arms, take away some of the tension and give him peace.

Where the hell had that come from? She was not a soft woman. The man broke into her house and she was here to scope him out as a possible murder suspect. Yet there was something here, just like last night, something more she could not begin to define.

"Chief Sarah," he said at last, a quirk to the corner of his mouth. "I like it."

"It's a liberty only afforded to senior citizens and people I like."

"Another reason to look forward to growing old. Would you like to come in, Chief? I admit, I'm surprised. You don't seem like the sex aid type."

"I thought one of those hopping penises would make a great stocking stuffer for my great-aunt."

"Sorry, none in stock. I've heard the local mall novelty store is selling them, along with velvet black light posters. Of course, you might be interested in the massages we offer on Tuesday nights for relaxation or stimulation." His expression remained bland. "Pedicures on Thursdays. With or without restraints. Your choice."

"I'm armed, Herne. Don't provoke me."

She wondered if he'd taken the time to shower and flushed, remembering his husky voice against her ear, promising to enjoy the feel of her juices drying on his testicles he drove home. She knew the convertible BMW in the lot was his, and so it made it impossible not to imagine him sitting in it just a few hours ago, her climax drying upon his genitals.

He stepped aside and let her pass into the open foyer. It was filled with an exotic scent, masculine and arousing all at once, like him.

Okay, so he'd created a classy façade. She didn't trust façades.

"Hmmm. Maybe you should try this." He picked up a frosted crystal atomizer and misted the base of her neck with it before she could duck away.

"Hey." She made herself, and the light aroma of peaches and lilies wafted up to her nostrils. An expensive, haunting fragrance, no cheap chemical odor. She liked it, but she frowned at him. "What is that?"

"Let me demonstrate how it works." He leaned forward, his eyes daring her to retreat. She firmed her jaw and her resolve and was annoyed to feel her pulse rate increase exponentially as he blew on her neck, his lips only a few inches away, his hair brushing her temple.

The skin beneath his breath grew pleasantly warm. "It has a delightful effect when used on nipples. Are you pierced, Chief? I can't seem to recall."

A pair of ladies stepped over the threshold, forestalling her retort.

Sarah made a note to find out if Lilesville had a dentist, because she was certain she had just ground the enamel off her bottom row of teeth. With a look that should have sliced off his legs at groin level, she stepped aside into the lingerie room to give him time to handle his customers.

The room was set up like an intimate boudoir. Silken sheer floor-length gowns that would have turned any woman into a lush Jayne Mansfield were displayed in an antique armoire, samples hung on the open doors. Scattered across a brass bed with a white eyelet coverlet were offerings of various bras, panties, camisoles and garters. Sarah's attention went to the wall beside the bed. In a mounted series of small curio cabinets, on crushed velvet under lighting that made things sparkle and catch the eye, were scrolled ben-wei balls and several varieties of bullet-shaped clitoral stimulators in silver or bronze. All were showcased in heart-shaped carved mahogany boxes and carried a five-year guarantee on workmanship. In the middle mirrored cabinet there were handcuffs, from polished police issue to those with a soft inner lining, both kinds resting on folds of soft blue gauze material, a stark contrast from how she usually saw handcuffs. Until this morning, when she had seen them on her bedspread, garnished with wildflowers.

Two privacy screens provided a changing area in a corner of the room, with a simple linen drape that would suggest the silhouette of the woman changing behind it.

Justin and his clients were moving toward the lingerie room, so Sarah stepped into the next display area, an old-fashioned washroom possessing a clawfoot tub with brass fixtures, a washstand and pedestal sink. Here she found the aromatherapy candles, arranged as if in preparation for the bather, lavender soaps, skin smoother creams, and other items to pamper and prepare the body to be touched. Interestingly, this was where Herne chose to display his adult book offerings. Sarah paged through a couple of the selections stacked artfully in the nook shelves above the tub and found erotic romances, geared to a woman's tastes. She read a few pages out of the middles, enough to tell her that Herne understood quite well that a woman's mind was the key to stimulating her body. No cheap pulp porn selections. A basket containing fluffy, fragrant towels was placed next to the tub. There was also an arrangement of waterproof vibrators and elegant shower head fittings with multiple settings in the same basket.

If a woman had this room and all its accoutrements at her disposal, why would she need a man? Sarah chuckled at the thought, though she immediately and vividly remembered Herne's touch on her body. The ravaging insistence of his mouth, his scent, his hunger, and her body's response to them. She knew the answer to the question, one that would reassure men everywhere. When a man took a woman the way she hungered to be taken, no machine could ever replace him.

She couldn't help but listen to the timbre of his voice, or notice from the corner of her eye how he reached out and slid his hand down the older woman's arm in a way that was entirely proper, and yet gentle and sensual at the same time. The woman looked like she was the age of Sarah's mother, but she blushed like a girl. Her rueful chuckle at herself only a second later suggested she had reached the point in her life where she could be comfortably amused with her reaction to a handsome man. Sarah envied it. Herne's knowing smile didn't seem smug, but a gesture of affectionate communication.

If it was an act on his part, it was one of the most well done she had seen. Herne looked genuinely attentive and focused on both women, pleased to have them there, not just to shop, but for the opportunity to meet them.

Good Lord, did the man splash himself in pheromones before he went out in the morning? Over several moments she watched his mouth curve in a near smile, straighten in attentive silence, then part in an offering of wisdom that gave her a flash of tooth and tongue. Her senses drowned out translation with the memory of that mouth on her breasts, her pussy, her own lips, and the thrust of that tongue into her body. The music of his voice was the sensual soundtrack against which she replayed the memory and imagined even more. She imagined herself lying unrestrained, twining and tightening her legs and arms around his lean and elegant body, instead of thrashing against her cold and unrelenting headboard railings.

She pushed away the fantasy and tuned in enough to listen to him encourage the bride to look at other options for her wedding night.

"Your first night of intimacy as man and wife should be given the same attention to detail you're giving to the more public aspects of the wedding," he said. He smoothly led them from the discussion of their original goal, the purchase of a suitable bridal nightgown, into decorations her attendants could take to prepare the bridal chamber. Rose petals, pillar candles, the proper music. He asked quiet, thoughtful questions that addressed the groom's as well as the bride's sexual likes and dislikes, the things they enjoyed in scents, music, intimacy. Sarah listened as an innocuous discussion of the bride's husband-to-be and his favorite choice of sweets led to Justin's recommendation of a smooth glitter body lotion that tasted like sugar cookies.

Jesus, women were as frank with him as their own doctor, telling him about their lover's preferences and interests. Like a physician, he prompted them in a professional, caring and yet authoritative manner, as if he had every right to know such things. Sarah could not help but be amazed at how he skillfully gleaned as much about the young woman's desires as her groom's by asking the right questions, and making the right comments at the appropriate times.

"Your likes are very important, Janet," he said, touching the woman's knee as she and her aunt sat in a pair of chairs in the boudoir around a hope chest fanned with catalogs of special order items. "A man truly in love will be most aroused by whatever arouses his lover. Men are voyeurs, and we love to watch a woman become aroused by the things we do to her."

"I told you he was marvelous." Her aunt nudged her and grinned at Justin. "Coming here to shop is as much fun as a full bridal shower."

Sarah decided she would just go ahead and move onto the next room to get a sense of the whole place before she found herself as mesmerized by the store's proprietor as his besotted clients. Her body tightened involuntarily as he chuckled at something the woman said, the sound stroking her like his fingers in her most sensitive areas.

Possible. Murder. Suspect. Sarah ground the three words out in her mind, forced her uncooperative body to listen. Man who trespassed in her home. Arrogant son of a bitch. Guy who provided her the best sex she'd ever had in her life.

Immaterial.

A plaque over the next doorway announced she was entering the playroom. There were no child-sized tables and chairs, or murals on the wall featuring trains and crayons, but there was play equipment. Sarah's fingers trailed over the rich red upholstery on a spanking bench, and she examined the restraint system on a chair that came with the option of several fittings to insert pleasurable objects into the body of the person reclined in it.

A double rack of costumes made up one whole wall. On an antique coffee table large books with glossy photos of role-playing suggested what costumes a client might choose. There were old style photos, like Rudolph Valentino with his harem girl, and modern day professional erotic art photography showing an impertinent maid over her Victorian master's knee. There was a female cop, well-endowed, leaning in the car window of an appreciative though nervous male. Her fingertips wrapped around the head of her baton in a suggestive manner that made Sarah's lips curve up.

The next room was a combination movie theater and art gallery. Movies had been grouped on the open, deep cushions of display sections of movie seats. Other titles lay at the base or propped against an old-fashioned projector. More were stacked in a pyramid on a counter that displayed candies beneath the glass that apparently were as much for sale as anything else in the room.

The framed erotic art dominated every available space on the walls, sponge painted in a soft green as a non-distracting, tranquil background. The art came from all different historic periods, from the Renaissance to modern day. She studied the subject matter, intrigued with Renaissance nudes as much as she was the modern day artistic renditions of the erotic. She cruised through some of the movie titles and found Sondergard, Fellini, Zalman King, Candide Royale, all apparently reputable cinematographers intrigued with the erotic.

There was another bathroom, laid out much like the first, and she was impressed that he would have thought to provide two areas, since the offerings in the bathroom would be popular but cramped to look over if too many customers were in the store. A second bedroom focused on the décor choices for the room in which lovers could get lost in one another for hours. Incense, bed linen choices, pillows, art, musical selections and a quality audio system to try out the different CDs. Sarah gave herself a shake to keep from getting absorbed in ideas for her own still relatively sparse bedroom.

This bedroom had a second door that gave her a partial view back to the lingerie room where he stood now, half turned away from her, talking to his two seated customers. Despite herself, Sarah's gaze lingered over him from her relatively screened position. His lower body, outlined so well in the dark pleated slacks, the lean muscles of his arms defined by their casual crossed position. His long fingered, clever hands folded against him. That sculpted face and hair soft to her touch. He had a shadow on his jaw, giving her the intimate knowledge that he had not had time to shave since he left her. She wondered what time he had left her and realized the dual implication of that important question.

A true cop, she let the scent of coffee draw her back to reality. The last room before she completed the circle back to the foyer was a kitchen and sunroom. As Eric had described, Herne had turned it into a cozy place to take a cup of coffee and a homemade sweet and look through other product catalogs or coffee table books. There was a bulletin board here and she noted he was offering Tantra classes and sensual massage, a lingerie fashion show and a creative cooking class, all about using food to enhance sexual interaction. There was a basket of brownies and jar of biscotti next to the full coffee urn. The wicker furniture in this room was grouped together in a cozy fashion and had bright print patterns on the cushions. The arrangement invited clients to stay and converse. There were other sale items in here as well, a selection of artwork, a rotating rack of more erotic romances and movies. A hallway tree draped with silk scarves in deep, sensual colors subtly implied that the scarves could be bought in groupings of four to use as restraints, or individually to decorate a lover's body.

With the full sunlight of this room, she recognized that each room she had visited had used light to create a mood. There had been filtered colored light from windows with stained glass, candlelight in the bathrooms, and dim light from elegant buffet lamps to create a relaxing and yet stimulating mood in each area.

Sarah suppressed a sigh. She was an astute cop, and she could not deny the obvious evidence. Everything here catered to a woman's desires. Eric was right. This wasn't a sex shop. It was a sensuality boutique.

Chapter 5

છ

Justin was not irritated to have Laura Crittenden and her niece interrupt his interaction with Sarah Wylde. It gave Sarah ample time to wander through his store, see what he was offering, form her impressions. He was certain she was carrying some fairly strong ones from last night, ranging from apprehensive to downright hostile. If she had been wearing a suit of armor when she stepped over his threshold, she could not be more obviously guarded against him.

He wondered if she knew how mesmerizing she was to watch. Like something magic discovered in a forest, and so she had been. Her face was reminiscent of a fairy creature, the skin stretched to almost transparency over her bones. Instead of making her look skeletal, the fineness of the bone structure was marvelous to study, inviting touch like the smooth curves of a work of sculpted art.

Her hair was a glorious tangle of white-gold, highlighting the soft mouse brown original color. It was full and fine at once, delicately wisping around her face and down her back when it wasn't pulled back for work.

Sometimes women in her line of work downplayed their femininity. While hers was so blatant he didn't think she could do it even if she tried, she didn't. Her nails were professionally manicured and painted a pale pink that matched her lipstick. Her jewelry was expensive and subtle. Small hoop earrings with a diamond and onyx inlay, and a slim gold bracelet watch. Her clothing folded against her shape and curves with the warm precision of a painting. Though the jeans and placket shirt were the casual uniform of the Lilesville police, he suspected all her clothes would have the simple, well-cut lines that neither added nor subtracted from the perfection of the female form.

She hadn't bothered with eye makeup this morning, but eyes like hers were strong enough to bring a man to his knees without enhancement. Her thin, sharp face had been blessed and enhanced by the deep set of a pair of large blue-gray eyes. He'd seen her picture in the paper when she was hired. She had worn a small amount of makeup, and it made those eyes even more startling and potent.

She wore one of those bras that made more of her bosom than was there, but he remembered her breasts quivering beneath his palms, and had been surprised at their fullness, given her build. He wondered how she would look in some of the nipple jewelry he had in the front foyer case. It brought an instant vision of her standing in the moonlight of her bay window, naked except for a silver serpentine chain and the sapphire beads strung on it to weight it, stimulating the nipples. Her breath would quicken as he drew the slack out of the chain, holding her still as he brought all that glorious hair tumbling over her pale, slender shoulders with his free hand.

He knew her to be more angular than curved, with a ridiculously tiny ass, and ribs he could feel under his palms. Despite that, everything about her screamed feminine, the way a willow tree did with its elegance and sweeping limbs.

He liked imagining her having those highlights put in her hair, having her nails done, adjusting her bra as she put it on in the morning so her figure was curvy and attractive, even as she then holstered her gun and that worry line marked her forehead between her brows as she considered the business of the day. A warrior goddess.

It wasn't just the gun that told him her nature. He knew something of her background, and in the dim light of her bedroom, he had seen the two places, felt them, his fingers tracing the shiny worn round scars over her kidney and next to her spine. Two bullet entry wounds that could have killed or permanently crippled her. He wondered if that was why she was here, then discarded the idea. If Sarah Wylde ran from anything, it wasn't physical danger, it was emotional pain. Even against that, he suspected she'd strike back as she had with him just now in his doorway, rather than retreat.

Maybe she didn't retreat enough.

She looked breakable, and yet there was strength in those eyes, the set of her jaw. She had a small mouth, and the way she held it closed and rigid reflected her stance to perform her job. Perhaps that was the way she was getting through this particular phase of her life.

Oh, he had the strongest case of instant attraction in his life since he had been in third grade and fell in love with his English teacher. That had been a mixture of physical and emotional attraction, mother and lover both. There was some of that here, too. This was more than physical. She was so touchable, tastable. He wanted to suck on each finger, kiss the skin of every crease of her, press his nose hard against all her parts, just to inhale her.

Great Lord, but she was one of the most beautiful women he had ever seen, and it was not an easily recognized or ordinary beauty. It called to him as strongly as the call between lifemates in the wild. This was something he wasn't going to leave alone, as much as he was sure she wanted him to do so.

Justin Herne revered women. He knew without any arrogance that he could sexually possess almost any woman whose heart was unclaimed. He knew how to touch them, how to listen without guile, and he had a pleasing face and form. He didn't use it unless it was for honest purposes. But what had happened in that small cottage on the edge of a dark forest defied anything he had ever experienced. He wanted to feel remorse or shame. That would be less disturbing than this drive to do it again, take her, hammer into her, overwhelm her defenses again and again until she accepted it, accepted him. He wanted to lose himself in her, in that sexual mystery that was this particular woman.

He certainly believed in unseen forces guiding Fate, but to have it so directly applying itself to his life in a way he had not anticipated or prescribed was very unsettling.

He left Laura Crittenden and her aunt reviewing some sample books and went back to the main glass counter. He waited for her to come to him.

* * * * *

When Sarah returned to the front foyer, Herne stood behind a glass counter, watching her. He had his admittedly fine ass braced against a stool, his legs stretched out before him, arms crossed over his chest. His eyes lingered on the swell of her breasts, the curve of her waist, the gun strapped to her side. His intensity gave her that animal sense of him again. He deliberately perused her as a lover, not a shopkeeper, and she knew he wanted her to be aware of it.

A moment of silence settled between them, and if he felt uncomfortable or nervous in her presence, he didn't show it. But did she really expect a man with the brazen confidence to trespass into the police chief's house and ravish her to be unsettled by "morning after" thoughts?

"You're like an elf," he said, startling her. "One of Tolkien's elves. Tall, slim, ethereal."

She'd had a metabolic disorder all her life, an inability to put weight onto legs, arms and a torso that shot out and up at an early age. When she was a child, her father called her his Black Beauty, then after the Academy, his Secretariat, his thoroughbred. She made sure the gristle that was there was tough muscle and contented herself with the knowledge she had two things that caught a man's eyes. Her hair and her boobs. Her lanky body hefted around a pair of beautifully shaped 36B breasts, a slightly large size for her underweight figure. Thank God they hadn't been Cs or Ds, or she would have looked like a freak. The weight would have toppled her forward.

"You have a wig missing off a mannequin head in your costume area," she said. "Was that a recent sale?"

"Shoplifter. They get past me sometimes when it gets busy in here. There's one on order to replace it."

She held his gaze a moment.

"So what inspired the shop? Figure it was a good way to pick up women, cater to all that stuff men really think is bullshit?"

"You could say that. But my favorite method of picking up dates is breaking into their homes after midnight."

"That's a dangerous thing for a man to admit to a cop," she retorted. "Mine is catching men with smart mouths speeding on back roads and beating the hell out of them."

"That's a dangerous thing for a cop to admit to anyone."

She would not laugh, she told herself firmly, no matter that the gleam in his eye had her wanting to do just that. "Don't you ever do any guy type things, Herne?" She swept her gaze over her surroundings, turning on her heel in a circle. "Arranging lingerie, conducting aromatherapy workshops. Don't you ever watch football, grunt, scratch your genitals like a normal male? Makes me kind of doubt there's a guy in there."

She turned around and he was right behind her, six inches separating the two of them. She hadn't heard him move from behind his counter, and could only conclude he sprouted wings and vaulted it. She managed to keep a nonchalant expression, though her pulse spiked to one-ninety.

"You're baiting me, Chief Sarah." His hand caught in her ponytail, and his hip pressed against her side. "And you're the only woman in a very, very long time, outside of a religious rite, who actually knows what's in my trousers."

Damn, he did that well. Asserted his testosterone and stroked her ego in one smooth movement. The man could conduct an orchestra with nerve like that.

He cocked his head. "You know, I have an ice blue silk teddy in there with sheer white stockings and heels dyed to match. The garters have jeweled clasps. You'd look gorgeous in it, Chief Sarah." His gaze coursed over her. "You'd look gorgeous in anything."

She arched a brow. Her attention had been caught by that particular garment over all the others in the lingerie room, so she hadn't gone anywhere near it. The man was an accomplished shopkeeper, that was all. "I suppose it has a thong back?"

He lifted a shoulder. "A male indulgence."

"I get hemorrhoids. Often. It would chafe."

A sparkle went through his beautiful eyes, making her suddenly, desperately wish she was here for some other reason. "It's the softest fabric imaginable. And I don't suppose I'd let you wear it long, anyhow."

Heat swept up straight from her center to her throat at that low, intimate voice. She'd never thought a man could purr. This one did. Not like a tame housecat, but like a mountain lion.

"Back off."

He deliberately lifted his hands, took two steps back behind his counter. Lacing his fingers together on the glass, he leaned forward, bringing that heady male cologne scent and his dark eyes to within six inches of her face. Even leaning forward, he was an inch taller than she was. She refused to back up, though every muscle tightened to painful rigidity, except her thighs, which had an infuriating tendency to loosen at his nearness.

"Tell me, Chief Sarah, how many respectable citizens of Lilesville do you think spent last night handcuffed to their beds, their kneecaps brushing their ears while they screamed for more?"

Anger management was part of cop training, but every officer learned to deal with it in his or her own way. Hers was visualization. In the space of three slow blinks she imagined in great detail taking Justin Herne by the neck, bashing his head through the display case and letting his unconscious body lie there sprawled among the delicate nipple chains and elegant slave collars.

The purple velvet one with teardrop diamonds and a yin yang silver pendant would look great with a cocktail dress she had. She noted it cost seventy dollars.

Sarah smiled at him. If she were a wolf, light would have glittered off her fangs.

"It happened, Herne," she said, taking a step forward so her hips were against the counter and they were nose-to-nose. She was proud to hear her words come out in an even, steady tone that she hoped matched the expression on her face. "Maybe it was more over the top than either of us expected it to be, and maybe that's making us both edgy." She straightened, stepped back. "We're adults. It's over, and I say we leave it at that."

I don't think so. It pissed him off, but not at her. His anger left, sliding down the same drain as hers.

He straightened, and it called to his mind two martial arts combatants, bowing at the end of a match that left each with an increased respect for the other.

"I'm sorry," he said. "You didn't deserve my crudity."

"I shouldn't have cursed at you, Mr. Herne."

A muscle flexed in his jaw. "I don't regret last night. In fact, I thought—"

"Don't think too much," she said, moving away as Laura and her niece came to the counter to discuss their order.

Wrong tactic. His police chief had shields, and she would erect them as fast as his cock was rising at the sight of her in her snug knit shirt and tan shoulder holster. Her jeans were not overly tight, but they hugged her ass and made him want to bite into the crotch, into the arousal he felt certain soaked the undergarment beneath. Her color was high, the pulse beating fast in her neck. During their exchange, her nipples had become prominent, despite the padding of her bra.

He had taken her down, this warrior who had trembled in his arms and made him forget anything but how much he wanted her.

He had been a Wiccan priest long enough to discern the difference between the post-high of ritual and the mundane planes. He had schooled himself to a rigid discipline of recognizing it, because it was too easy to get lost in the euphoria of Their power. When he came into her home, the lingering awareness of the Rite had brought him the strong smell of her arousal, his elevated animal instincts honing in on her. They let him know she would open to him, and a part of him had seized the knowledge, ridden up and over any civilized veneer he pretended to have, because *she was his*. Theirs was a true call of flesh to flesh, whether it be in the service of the Lord and Lady, or just for a strong powerful fucking, a mutual possession. He even felt it this morning at the sight of her, the smell of her. She hadn't showered yet. The surge of possession was so strong it had made him turn nasty, go for the low blow. *His* warrior goddess.

He doubted she had much interest in the crotchless panties she was fingering, but they were producing some delightful images in his mind. By the Goddess, there were times that his choice of profession was a detriment. He was glad for the plywood door at the back of the display case, otherwise his erection would have put to shame any sexual aid in the store and likely scared Laura and her niece into the next county. He managed a focused and warm smile for them as he gave them their receipt for their special order items, but he knew he wasn't fooling the older woman. Laura's gaze flickered between him and Sarah's rigid back, and she had a knowing smile as she and Janet took their leave, wandering out onto the porch with comfortable female chatter and the expected giggles about the gargoyle.

Sarah did not immediately turn around, even as they left the porch and made their way into the parking lot. Her fingers still rested on the silk of the panties, absently moving as if she was using her repetitive strokes on the soft texture to soothe herself. She didn't realize that there was a small mirror on the far wall for checking out jewelry choices. If she had known, he was sure she would not have allowed him to see her staring off into space, a bleakness in her eyes.

"Do you have a faith, Chief Sarah?" he asked quietly.

Her shoulders tensed. "Why would you ask that?"

"Because I think you do, and you seem a little disappointed in it right now."

"Well, most things don't live up to your expectations."

"Last night did." He watched her still profile, the fair brow and straight set of her firm mouth. "I'm hard as a rock now, just thinking about it."

She did turn now, her eyes remote. "You're a pretty savvy salesman, Herne." She jerked her head toward the parking lot. "She comes in here to buy some skimpy nighty to impress her groom and you've got her paying for a whole production number."

"Tell me, Chief, do you always whip out the jaded cop routine to shore up your defenses, or do you have something more fresh and original?"

Sarah stiffened. "About as original as dodging an accusation with a personal insult."

He pressed his lips together, and she had the distinct impression he was suppressing amusement. "Very good," he said. "Well then, I guess I could mention that their first joining is supposed to be sacred."

"Do you think, for anybody getting married these days, it's the first time?"

"It's their first time as husband and wife, lifetime mates. That makes it sacred, and special." He leaned back against the stool, crossed his arms again in that way that drew her eye to the fine lines of his upper body. "Yes." He nodded. "It does bring me more sales if they see it that way, but it also gives them something as well. The marriage ceremony will pass in a haze of apprehension of last minute details." His eyes widened and his voice altered to mimic a breathless bride. "Will Grandpa So-n-So get drunk at the reception? Will the caterers remember to pour the champagne at just the right time?"

His voice returned to its normal tone, and he pinned her with the intensity of those dark eyes. "That night, when it's just the two of them, that will be the first time it will sink in, those vows they exchanged. Not just the words, but the meaning beneath them. They'll know from here forward, it's the two of them." He blinked, once. "A good salesperson only sells a person what they truly want, and what will benefit their lives. If you do anything else, you're no better than Dr. Feelgood, peddling his sugar-water cure-alls."

"Until what God has brought together, time and job stress rend asunder." She fought to draw a breath against the fist squeezing the air from her lungs.

"Is that what happened to you, Sarah? Your man couldn't handle being married to a cop? Or you couldn't figure out how to lower the shields when you left the office?"

She took a step back into the cozy coffee room. She had a brief impression of his expression, of his arrogance and annoyance with her changing to something else, but she didn't want to see it. She turned away, overwhelmed by feelings gone from flatline to overdrive, galvanized by the truth of his words like the slamming pressure of a foot on the gas pedal of a race car.

"Sarah—" he was right behind her.

"If you touch me, I'll break your fucking fingers. I swear to God I will."

She felt his hands hovering just outside her shoulders, their aura of heat awakening her skin. He withdrew. She knew he didn't fear her threat. Somehow he understood how vital it was to give a person the space to collect shattered shields and lash them back together. She wondered what had happened to him that he knew that.

"I came to get you," she said, turning to face him. She knew her face was too tense, too pale, from the look of concern in his eyes. *Don't be sensitive, I'll fly apart. Be an asshole. Make him one.* "Police business."

It took him a moment to digest that, change gears. "Last night? Sarah—"

"No. Not exactly." She hoped. It would be beyond a nightmare if he was somehow involved in this murder, and he had been in her bed. She wished he would call her Chief Wylde, wished she had the right to make him do so. She wanted to march past him and leave, but that was no longer an option.

"I'm here to ask your help on a case, if you're up for it."

He looked startled, and it gave her some satisfaction to keep him off-balance. "I can't imagine what crime could have occurred in Lilesville that would require my expertise."

"It's in Marion, just over the line. It looks like a ritual murder."

It didn't hit him at first, and she knew that was a point in his favor, unless he was a better actor than she thought he was.

"A murder, here?"

"Maybe. We're not sure. I figure you might be our resident expert on some of the paraphernalia that was used. This hasn't hit the press yet. We've kept it off the radios. We want to identify the victim first."

"You want...the body is still there?"

Color drained from his face. Sarah mentally cursed herself. In a small town, murder was not an everyday thing, and no matter how together Justin Herne had been in her bedroom, what she saw now was a rattled civilian. She would have done more handholding if she were asking anyone else to go look at the scene as an expert. A prime example of why it was so easy for the personal to fuck with professional judgment.

"Hey. " She made herself reach out, touch his hand which had clenched into a white-knuckled fist at his side, an unconscious reaction of defense. It wasn't as hard as she expected it to be. She had to suppress the unusual desire to lace her fingers in his and create a stronger link. "I could really use your help. I won't make you get any closer than you feel like getting. You don't—" She bit back impatience with herself. "I can't make you do it. You have a choice. You're just quicker than calling someone in from Gainesville."

He looked down at their hands, and he surprised her by turning his over and closing his fingers around her smaller hand. His strength was there, but unsteady, as if he drew some of hers into him from their shared touch. He took a deep breath and suddenly she understood.

She knew that look, had seen it on faces before. This wasn't the first time he'd seen someone dead from violent means, and it hadn't been long for him, if that gray pallor under the skin meant anything.

"No." He shook his head, pulled his hand away. "If I can help, I will. We're a community here, Chief. Whoever this is, he or she deserves any help we can give. Let me just post a sign on the door and lock up before we go. I'd rather you drive, if you don't mind."

Chapter 6

ഌ

The drive to the murder site was awkward. In the silence, Sarah regretted her sniping comments. He hadn't deserved it. Oh, maybe he had, the way he had bowled her over, but his tension was palpable next to her. It was her job to deal with it.

"You have a nice place, Mr. Herne." There. She had been pleasant, though it was an effort.

He made a noise, somewhere between a snort and a faint chuckle. "*Mr. Herne.* I've never been on such formal terms with a lover before."

She stomped the brake, bringing them to an abrupt halt on the rural highway, and glared at him. "We're not lovers, Herne. We had a quick fuck and that was it. It was a mistake in judgment on my part, and if you don't drop it, it's going to be a serious mistake in yours."

He studied her. "Is that why you looked at me the way you did at the shop, when you thought I wasn't looking? Because I was a quick fuck?" He turned back to the window. "I must look like hell if you're trying to be nice to me."

He was hard to keep up with. Sarah tried counting to ten for patience, made it to five. "I'm normally a nice person. You bring out the mean in me."

He smiled, but his attention was on something far beyond the car.

"So why this kind of store? Why not just your average sex shop? You know, no windows, dirty books, fluorescent lights and all male clientele?"

"Well, when you make it sound so appealing, I can't imagine what came over me," he said dryly. He spread his fingers out, long and capable, on his knees. "The easy answer is I enjoy women. A woman's desires have always fascinated me, so different from ours."

She'd hit the right button. The store was as much about who he was as it was his livelihood, which was obvious from walking into it. She didn't want to think about whether she'd done it to pump him for information or to get his mind off of what lay ahead. She supposed it didn't matter as long as it accomplished the same thing.

"How so?"

He slanted a glance at her, and she thought he knew what she was doing, because a look of amusement crossed his features, as if he were laughing at both of them.

"Sexuality for women is such a deep, spiritual part of them, connected to the sacredness of the Earth herself. Male sexuality is the curiosity of the rover, the passion of the hunter, the bird flashing into the sky in a sudden burst of exuberance. It's woman's body that grounds him, that brings above and below together and balances. To find ways to bring forth that deep sensuality in a woman to make it easier for the two to come together, that's a sexual experience surpassing anything a casual rut with the campus cheerleader can bring."

"So your faith is a 'make love not war' type of thing?"

He did not smile this time. "It's easy to think of it that way, more harmless. That only touches on the surface of some very deep waters. The Goddess is as much warrior as creator." His gaze moved to her badge clipped on her belt, her gun in the shoulder holster. "You know that."

They pulled onto the service access road. Justin blinked. "You didn't say this adjoined my property."

"You didn't ask, and I didn't know for sure, though I suspected. You've got a pretty sizeable chunk of land. We have to park here and walk a ways. It's marked with tape." She glanced at his polished shoes. "Sorry. I should have warned you we'd be going through the woods."

"It's all right." He got out, bent out of sight behind the door. When he came around to join her, he was barefoot, carrying the shoes in one hand, the socks folded inside them.

He should have looked silly, but he didn't. Instead, she was reminded forcefully of what he had looked like in the woods the previous night, bare except for the antlered headdress. She recalled also that the shoes in his hand were the ones he had worn less than a few hours ago while he knelt on her bed, driving into her.

He'd caught her staring. That knowledge started her from her musings, warmed her cheeks.

"Aren't you worried about the slacks?" She gestured toward the expensive summer wool.

"Do you want me to take them off?"

It was a sardonic comment, without humor. He apparently wasn't feeling like laughing, at her or with her.

"Sorry, I wasn't thinking of it that way. Come on."

He followed her to the murder site without another word. When they got to the lip of the shallow valley where the victim was located, Sarah saw the scene through his eyes. The dark earth, the pale, uncovered body, the staring eyes. She glanced at him, studied his face as both cop and lover. She acknowledged the necessity of the duality at the same time she regretted it, though she wasn't yet sure which one caused her the most chagrin.

Up until his face changed, when she told him what she wanted him to do, she realized she had felt as though he had the upper hand, that he was untouchable, not human. A woman was allowed to be a bit touchy and defensive around a man who had overwhelmed her every defense. Maybe that's why now she felt so much more kindly disposed toward him.

He had paled again, but the set of his jaw was grim and he didn't turn away. He appeared frozen, every muscle of his body locked. His pulse pounded visibly in his throat.

There was a uniform overseeing the site with Eric, but they weren't doing much, just waiting for her to bring Herne to view the body before they removed the victim. "No press yet?" Sarah asked.

Chief Wassler shook his head. "We're out in the middle of nowhere, and so far we've kept it off the radio. I'll do a press release after the coroner picks her up. Justin, good to see you. Thanks for coming."

Herne nodded, his mouth a thin line. Sarah let him take the lead, subtly motioning Eric to hang back with her as they approached the ritual site and the woman's body. She kept to Herne's left so she could see his profile. As he got closer his face grew more empty and still, as if he were mimicking the corpse's lack of animation. When he swallowed and went glassy-eyed, she prepared to leap forward and push his head between his knees before he keeled on her. Then she saw his eyes start moving. She could almost hear the wheels clicking, as they had for her when she viewed her first victim. *Focus on the clues, the evidence, portion it down so you don't lose your mind or your stomach.*

"This is a typical circle casting," he said at last. His voice was rough and strange. Sarah saw his jaw had not relaxed a fraction, his gaze still on that white, motionless body.

"She most likely used a dark, dry dirt to cast the circle and pentagram. It's a good ingredient, because you can do a liberal coating but it will blow away and remix with the earth, less clean up. She'll have called the quarter spirits, names for the four elements that would have suited her purpose. That's what the oak branch, candle, censer and goblet represent. Four of the nine stones mark them, the others for the five points of the pentagram, as you can see. If there are carvings on them they may be symbols you'll want me to see and identify. They could be bindings, to hold whatever she called in, or reinforcements for the spell she was casting." He swallowed again. "The cat's blood was to help call it."

He closed his eyes.

Sarah cursed herself, gave in and put a hand on his arm. "Can you take a closer look at the body?"

Justin raised his lids, looked at her as if she were speaking a foreign language. "Yes, I can," he said.

He took the necessary eight steps to draw near her, and Sarah could almost feel how difficult each of those steps was for him. She and Eric stayed close behind him, exchanging a glance.

Justin stopped, looked down. "May I touch her?"

Sarah turned to the uniform and he provided a pair of latex gloves. "You can, but wear these. And give me your shoes."

He hesitated, nodded and made the exchange. Inevitably, their fingers brushed, and his eyes flickered up to hers.

Sarah held his gaze with a flat expression of her own. She could keep the impassive cop face in their present surroundings, but it was harder than usual. He turned away, put on the gloves and knelt by the body.

He touched her face, traced the sunken cheeks, the drawn lines around the mouth. "She's not this old," he said.

"She shows evidence of being a hard drug user," Sarah began, but he shook his head again.

"No, it's not that. Something sucked the life from her."

A chill skittered up Sarah's spine. "Are you suggesting she called some type of vampire?"

"If I did, I'm sure you wouldn't believe it. I'm telling you I knew this woman."

Sarah came to attention and felt Eric do the same. "How did you know her?" Wassler asked.

"Her name is Lorraine Messenger. She's in her early thirties. She moved to the county area about three months ago. I don't know where she was living, if she was living anywhere. She approached me about joining our coven. It was obvious her addiction made her unstable. I told her..." He stopped, and for a moment Sarah could not see his face, because he averted it, stared at the woods. "She would not be permitted to join our coven unless she took steps to clean herself up. I offered to get her into a program. She declined, and I didn't see her again."

He rose, turned back to Sarah. When strong emotions seized him, she realized that all those perfect features grew still. His dark eyes seemed to go flat and yet fathomless at once, and Sarah felt as if she could be lost in the abyss of their desolation.

"The blood painted on her arms and legs is likely hers. The cat's was used to strengthen the outer circle. Your own blood is the most powerful binding agent. She was calling something to her specifically," he said.

"Was there anybody else here with her? Based on your experience with that type of ritual?"

"It's best to do with at least one other person. When you're calling spirits from the astral planes, you can run into trouble. It's like going swimming by yourself. If you get in too deep, there's no one to pull you out or run for help. But she might have done it by herself, if she was unwise."

He motioned to their surroundings. "The center of the pentagram, the pentagon she's in here, next to the fire, this was where she intended to contain what she called." He nodded toward the portion of black powder that had been scattered. "There's where it broke through and left her after it killed her. From her appearance, whatever it is froze her to death."

Sarah heard the uniform murmur behind her and tried not to let the same incredulity she heard in his tone reflect in her voice. "You're serious. You think...whatever she summoned did this to her?"

"I know it. You won't find any evidence of another human being at this site, Chiefs. I promise you that."

She'd been fucked half-blind by a lunatic, a Twilight Zone escapee who likely believed in alien abductions.

"So, what was it?" She'd play along and see what she could learn.

"I'm not sure." He hesitated, then pointed at Lorraine Messenger's midriff. "There's a tattoo of a seal there, a sigil. It might represent what she called." He lifted a shoulder. "I can research it and let you know what it represents. I know you don't believe my theory, Chief. You said I'd be useful to you for my ritual knowledge, so you can use it or not, and discount the rest as the ravings of a lunatic, if it makes you sleep better at night."

"There are things you're not telling me," she realized.

"Many things, Sarah." His gaze came back to hers, and she felt the heat rise in her face. "But they're things you wouldn't believe and aren't ready to hear. What you need to know about this woman's death, I've told you."

"Cops tend to like to decide for themselves what they need to know. You know the charge for obstruction, Herne?"

"There are penances of the soul that are far more harsh to bear than the longest prison sentence." He gazed down at Lorraine Messenger again. "You are looking at someone who has paid hers.

"You've no reason to trust me, Chief Sarah," he added quietly. His attention went to Wassler. "But believe me when I tell you what else I know about this woman is simply the sad story of a wasted life, with no bearing on your investigation."

"And, regardless, it's all you're going to tell us."

"Yes. I'm sorry. The rest should be between her and the Goddess. I would like to give her a final blessing."

"Why?" Wassler frowned.

"I am a priest of my faith, and this woman was of that faith."

Sarah glanced at Eric, gave him a slight nod. The Marion police chief grunted, took out a cigarette and stepped away, nodding his reluctant agreement.

Justin knelt, pressing his fancy slacks into the earthen floor at the woman's side. He took Lorraine Messenger's right hand in the gentle grip of his gloved one. He bowed his head and began to murmur words Sarah could not hear. She felt that heat gather around him, like the blast from the circle she had experienced the night before. It was a different heat from what she had felt in her home. That had been an intimate energy between the two of them. This was magic and power, and the difference disturbed her. She would have preferred not to discern the difference, so she could claim Herne had used some hocus-pocus on her, rather than just brought out something in her that readily accepted him into her bed. Something that she felt even now with every look he shot her way, every time his scent reached her nostrils, or his body brushed hers in the most casual contact.

She turned to Wassler.

"At least we have an ID, and that's a start," the chief commented, tearing his gaze from Herne. He didn't look any happier than Sarah did.

"Yeah, but he's not telling us everything he knows," she murmured.

"You still think he might have done this."

"No, actually, I don't, but I think he might suspect who did." At Eric's narrowed expression, she put a hand out to stay him. "And I don't think it's some demon from another plane. You know him better. I won't tell you your business, but if it were me, I'd take him down to your office and grill him for a while, try to get it out of him with a duty-to-the-community approach." She turned so her back was to Herne and drew Wassler a few steps further away. "Have your investigative team head over to Gainesville and see if they can use the department's computers to run any connections between Justin Herne and Lorraine Messenger. Sometimes if you can wiggle your toe in through the door of the room where the witness or suspect is hiding their information, they'll give in and open up."

She turned at a rustle of leaves. Justin rose to his feet. "If you're done with me, I'd like to go home. I can walk from here. There's a trail to my house just over that rise."

It was pretty ballsy of him to draw their attention to it, Sarah thought. He'd have made a good cop, Eric was right, except for the fact she now thought his polished shoe tips hadn't brushed the tallest grass blades of the ground of reality in awhile.

"I'd like to talk to you down at my office for a bit, Justin," Wassler said. "Go over some of the things you talked to Sarah about."

"All right." Justin nodded. "But I'd like to go home for about an hour. I can bring you some books and printouts that will confirm what some of this means, give you some other sources on it. Will that work?"

"That'll be fine," Eric said after a glance at Sarah. She stood impassively, letting him take the lead on that decision. "My office in an hour."

Justin nodded, accepted his shoes from Sarah. He turned away, stopped. "You already solved one crime today, officers."

"What's that?" Sarah asked, brow raised.

He glanced back at her, and she thought a ghost couldn't look as transparent and haunted as he did.

"That's my wig she's wearing, the one missing from my shop."

He walked out of the circle, away from the body and them, his back tense. He took the trail up the ravine side with familiar confidence, but as he came out of the shadows at the top of the rise, Sarah noticed his shoulders had slumped, his control slipping. He'd done well, better than a lot of rookies with their first body. Sarah had the absurd desire to follow him, to be there to help make sure he could handle what he had just seen.

Where had the flash of tenderness come from? She hadn't acted so stupid over a guy since she was fourteen.

She knelt, looked at the tattoo he had mentioned. It was on the woman's belly, just over the womb, and it was new. The skin was still irritated around it and the colors were vibrant, a swirling pattern that made no sense to Sarah.

A drug addict in a Florida forest, wearing a three-digit wig, sporting a new tattoo and looking like she had died of exposure on an Alaskan tundra. If Marion was going to have its first murder since pioneer days, why couldn't it have been a flash of barroom temper, a domestic dispute instead of a Thomas Harris novel?

She just couldn't see Justin as Hannibal Lecter.

Chapter 7

ℬ

She filled out a report, met with the Lilesville town manager to fill him in on what she knew, and did the same with her men. There was the usual business of traffic issues, animal control calls and the occasional squabble over a parking space or petty vandalism that made up typical police work in a small town.

As she moved through her day, a strange collage of thoughts stayed with her. Lorraine Messenger's vacant eyes, the sigil tattoo, Justin's smooth voice offering a bride guidance, a black powdered circle, the charred remains of a bonfire. Justin's body covering hers, surging into her and slamming into her defenses, knocking them down one by one like dominos until she had nothing separating her soul from his except the smashed ruins.

Another person would have discounted such a strange grouping of thoughts to mental agitation from the murder, or indigestion. Sarah knew better. The images were linked somehow, and it was her job to find out how. Eric Wassler's call gave her the excuse, though she didn't welcome it.

"Sarah, Eric here. I've talked to the coroner and the guys in Gainesville, but they had two college girls murdered up there last night, and they've already told me pretty bluntly the of a junkie drifter in our little county isn't going to be put ahead of those two girls. They're saying it could be the end of the week or next week before we get any reports from the data we gave them.

"As far as Herne goes, he's a cagey bastard. I didn't get any more out of him than you did, but you're right, I think he has information he's not sharing. If it's not too much to ask, since he's in your town, dog him a bit this week for me. Maybe the new kid on the block will have better luck. I'll keep after the Gainesville boys."

Not too much to ask, unless you wanted to avoid the man in question at all costs.

She found herself going back down the drive to *For Her* at four thirty. Only his car was in the parking lot. She'd hoped to question him between the distractions of customers again. She hesitated, her engine idling, then cursed herself for it, for her hesitation and her desire to avoid being alone with him had nothing to do with the job. She switched off the engine and deliberately strode up to the door, slamming the screen on her way in.

The front foyer area was empty.

"I'll be right with you." Herne's voice came from somewhere above, up a cordoned-off staircase, blocking the way to the inventory in the attic, she supposed.

Sarah wandered into the lingerie area. He had moved the ice blue teddy from its display area on the armoire and had it hanging on the privacy screen. Had someone else tried it on? She noticed it was her size.

She glanced around, touched the watered silk. It shimmered like moonlight on ice. Tiny pearls had been worked into the lace of the neckline, and there was padding and wiring to push up and out what you had, that delightful overflowing tavern wench look that was the joy and awe of every small-breasted woman.

"I was going to send it to you as a gift."

He was right behind her. When she turned, he stood inside her personal boundaries.

"I came back to buy it for a date I have this weekend," she said, her eyes cool and remote. "Cops don't accept bribes."

"And here I figured you had come back to see if you could pry the answers out of me that Chief Wassler couldn't get." He leaned forward, bringing his shoulder within touching distance of her lips, slipped the garment off the ivory quilted hanger and handed it to her. When she drew in his smell, it hit her like a sensual caress to her internal organs. "You'll want to try it on, then."

There was nothing in his expression but the well-meaning concern of the professional shopkeeper, though she noticed he did not remove himself physically from her even one inch. His dark eyes were as intimate in their regard as the garment clutched in her hand. "Make sure it fits your body as well as the man for whom you're wearing it. It's $150 and lingerie is non-refundable. That's quite a lot to risk on a cop's salary." His eyes glinted. "Especially if she doesn't take bribes."

He motioned toward the screen. Trapped, Sarah set her jaw. Fine. She'd go in, put it on, tell him it didn't fit.

Only it did. When she slid the teddy on, it fit so perfectly she relented to the inevitable purchase and slid her panties off so she could see the trim line of it from waist to crotch. The thong back was soft, a stimulating friction between her cheeks as he had told her it would be. The shaping of the wired cups gave her bosom a lift so awesome she couldn't resist trailing her fingers in amazement over the plump curves of their tops. A movement snapped her gaze to the mirror.

"Hey," she said, whirling around to confront Herne, watching her over the screen.

"I've seen you in less," he pointed out, and came around to place the matching shoes on the floor. He went to one knee. "Hold onto my shoulder and step into them."

Sarah deliberated on whether she should just plant her foot in his chest and knock him on his ass. Instead, she ignored his shoulder and braced herself on the wall for balance to slip into the soft gloved feel of the three-inch pale blue heels.

Herne guided her second foot into the shoe, his touch lingering on her ankle and drifting up her calf. He raised his head slowly, and she watched his gaze cover the slope of her thighs, the barely covered mound of her pussy, the curve of her belly and the rise of her breasts. By the time he got to her face, her breath was shallow. He rose, so close his leg and hip brushed hers. His arm slid around her hips, the fingertips of his other hand trailing up her bare left thigh. "You look beautiful, Sarah," he said, his voice as soft as a stroke of fur. "No. More than that. You look irresistibly fuckable."

Her heart jumped in panic. *Get a grip, officer.*

"Well, I hope the guy I'm wearing it for will think so."

"Sarah." The small area behind the screen became even more so with just that one murmured word, the heat and steel that transformed his expression. They made her even more aware of everything the garment revealed. The cool air of the shop on her exposed breasts, the press of the thong strap against sensitive nerve endings in dark, secret places, the way the cotton crotch rubbed her dampening folds as she shifted. The tightening of the satin ribbon straps on her bare shoulders as she took a shuddering breath. Her legs trembled when his hands closed on her waist. She jolted at the sensation that swept through her at that one point of contact.

Her lips moistened, parted. "What?"

She meant to sound tough, unaffected. Instead, she sounded as if she could be shoved to her back by the touch of a finger. If that finger were Justin Herne's it might be more truth than metaphor.

"You're a liar."

He twisted his fingers in the strap on the left shoulder and yanked it down, exposing her breast to the eager cup of his palm. Sarah gasped and arched into his touch, and found her mouth claimed by his. His arm around her waist hauled her up against the full length of his body. He lifted her on her toes so her heels rose out of the shoes.

With a man as elegant and smooth as Justin Herne, a woman expected intimacy to be a well-planned ballet. Sarah knew he was capable of it. But when he moved to kiss her now, he was quick, brutal, overpowering. In a hungry and terrifying heartbeat she realized he had laid a claim on her and this was his reminder of it, a warning that there were consequences to provoking him.

She had never kissed a man who kissed like Justin Herne. Hell, she had never imagined a man could kiss like this man did. He used not just his lips, but his hold on her body to enhance the effect and make it explosive. He held her relentlessly against him as his hand moved up from her breast to her jaw, his thumb against her throat, collaring and caressing her at once. Her bare nipple pressed into the soft cotton of the black T-shirt while his hand splayed out so his fingers could stroke the dip into the valley between her buttocks. He nipped the thong strap in his fingers and tugged, making her moan into his mouth and rub her mound against him for a sweet burst of friction she felt thrum through her thighs and lower belly.

Then there was his mouth, tongue and teeth, scraping, licking, sucking and nibbling until she could only hold on, her body too weak to do more. She didn't believe in this kind of magic. Every brain cell screamed one word.

More.

* * * * *

She had a date. Like hell she did. Chief Sarah hadn't opened her legs or her heart to anyone since her divorce, he'd bet his store on it. The pussy he'd had the pleasure of enjoying last night had been excruciatingly tight. Her prickly attitude told him her heart was in the same condition.

Cops weren't normally a trusting group, and one recently ditched in a marriage would not be an easy fortress to storm. It was a good thing he'd done extensive reading on the strategies of medieval sieges for a history term paper in college. It was going to take a complex plan not only to take this castle, but to keep it. Driving the battering ram through the door to keep it open for a full invasion seemed a logical first step.

His grip eased, but only to spin her around so she faced the window next to the mirror. One arm remained clamped around her waist. This part of the house faced away from the road, toward a small lawn where spring wildflowers were starting to come up, bathed in gold by the late afternoon sun, and outlined by the acres of verdant green marsh and silver water of high tide just beyond them. Sarah caught the edge of the frame and closed her eyes as his fingers tugged at her ponytail and brought her hair spilling onto her shoulders.

"Glory," he murmured, and dropped her barrette to the floor. His fingers slid over her thighs, under the narrow silk and lace crotch, and gently he stroked her damp folds.

"Justin," she managed. "You can't—"

"Sshh…" His nose pressed into her hair. He began a slow, painstaking process of using the movements of his face against her to spill her hair forward and bare her neck. Each small shove to move the strands to the edge of her shoulder and send them tumbling forward onto her breast was accompanied by a soft nuzzle, a lick or a gentle bite of her nape. His thumb made idle passes on her clit, dipping and pressing slightly into her pussy, making her ass lift in response and slide against his erection, pushed against her. Still he took his time, worrying her neck. She began to wish she had less hair, and then more, and then she was incapable of deciding whether she wanted him to stop, or if she could never get enough.

At last he rubbed his rough jaw against her skin, and his nose into the shallow dip of her collarbone, so her head fell back against his shoulder, letting him suckle the taut line of her windpipe, which seemed to be processing far too little air. His hand took hold of her bare breast, not the nipple, the whole thing, as if he cradled a fragile treasure beneath which her heart beat rapidly.

"I know this may be hard for you to believe, Sarah," he said, low, his breath hot against her skin. "I didn't come to your home last night to ravish you. But once I saw you, smelled you, I had to have you. That was personal, Sarah. We *are* lovers." His hand tightened on her, not so gentle. "It's not about time or preparation. It's a spark, ignited in a single moment, and don't you dare deny it. You know when it happened last night, as much as I do."

She did remember, though she had tried to block it, even denied it to herself when the moment had occurred last night. Their faces had been close, and he had been inside her. They had both grown still, as if suddenly time stopped, and there was a heavy haze of desire slowing their movements. He had lowered his lips to hers, not to plunder but to sip, to taste and find *her*, and offer himself. It had been there, an all-consuming moment of heart, mind and soul, and though it had slipped away before the power of their lust only a blink later, it had been potent enough to embed itself in her memory, called up the moment he summoned it now. It had been intimacy, uncalled but imposing itself on them all the same.

He slid back and began to kiss her, working his way down her spine.

"Do you know how many vertebrae there are, Sarah?"

"No," she rasped.

"Eight cervical, twelve thoracic, five lumbar and five sacral vertebrae...and then there is the coccyx, the lovely, lovely tailbone."

His mouth closed over one of the bumps of bone he had enumerated for her, licked. Then another. "I do not want to miss a single...perfect...one...of them. Ah...missed that one. Have to start over."

Sarah whimpered. His thumb pushed more deeply into her pussy as he went several inches back up her spine and started down again. He was everywhere on her. A wet warm mouth, a flick of the tongue on her spine. A slow, circular stroke of his thumb inside her cunt. The firm hold of that arm banded across her, his palm holding her breast, kneading it. What was it about a strong man holding a woman helpless back against him that could make the knees weak and all brain cells leave the skull?

"Justin," she pleaded. Her body shook like a newborn colt. An orgasm was rising in her in a way she had never experienced before, a slow tide rolling in from the horizon. She felt it coming, not in a furious rising crest, but a straight, powerful charge that would punch into her lower body and knock her legs out from under her.

"Darling Sarah. Let me hear you. I love to hear you come."

Counting down another vertebrae in a whisper, his hand worked her. Her pussy made a succulent noise, the juices so thick they dampened her thighs and his knuckles. His trousers rubbed against her bare cheeks, exposed by the thong. The hard outline of his cock was firmly wedged in the channel between her buttocks, pushing the thong strap deeper into her cleft, and her instinctive movements stroked him against her anus, the rhythm working at odds with his hand as her hips rose and fell with her erratic breathing. She kept coming down on his thumb, which was now pushed inside her to the farthest knuckle, that curve of bone resting firmly against her clit. His other fingers were insinuated between her thighs, braced out straight and unrelenting against them so she had to stay spread open, unable to contain or control the building climax.

He straightened and brought his lips back to her neck. His body pressed fully against hers, giving her a shock of emotional intimacy that shoved the physical response up another notch.

"No."

She barely got it out, but managed to let go of the sill, trusting him to hold her up with the arm banded around the front of her body. Sarah closed her hand over his large one between her legs. "No. I want you inside, Justin. Inside."

He stilled, eased his thumb from her, nipping her neck as she groaned at the sensation. She twisted in his arms and fumbled for the buckle of that slim, elegant belt holding up his neat trousers. The head of his cock rubbed against her wrists through the summer wool. He muttered an oath, relenting, and helped her, stripping off the belt and unfastening the clasp, shoving the pants and the underwear beneath down to his thighs.

He caught her under the arms before she could touch him and lifted her onto the sill, her shoulder blades against the hard wood of the pane dividers and cool glass. The motion was rough but effective, his cock finding her slippery opening and plunging into her in a movement so immediate she screamed at the sensation. Her legs lifted, wrapped around him, and she banded her arms around his shoulders, wishing she could feel his skin. She settled for the press of her temple and cheek against his soft hair, and drew in the smell of him with all the mysterious scents of his shop.

He caught her arms and lifted her upper body away from him. "Tell me, Sarah," he said, his face harsh with need, more than the need of the moment. "Tell me you want me."

She shook her head, made to pull him to her again, but he had the belt in his right hand. He shifted his grip to hold it against her upper body, the strap pressed horizontally from shoulder to shoulder, pinning her against the window. It was positioned right above her nipples, the tension causing the stiffened points to tilt upward and constricting the blood flow so her breasts instantly became more sensitive. He had his hips pressed hard in between hers, his cock and his body working with the immovable wall to keep her still. His eyes on hers, he lowered his head, suddenly back to being slow, and flicked one nipple with his tongue.

She cried out. The nerve endings reacted as if jolted with electric current. Her lungs pumped for air against the restrictive hold of the belt while he began to suckle her gently, as if he had all the time in the world. He kept his hips still, even though her own struggled to move on him, to get some friction going between her pussy and the thick cock he had buried in her. It moved just a bit within her with the movements of his upper body as he devoted himself to nursing her breast, his mouth making soft, wet noises against her nipple. There was a coil of energy so tight in her lower body that the waves rippled out through her thighs, tiny orgasms that hinted at the power of a full onslaught.

He traced the curve of her breast with his tongue, moved like a slow tide toward the other eager flushed point. Just her watching the progress of his tongue made the nipple stiffen further. He blew on it, giving it heat, then closed over it and began to suckle again.

"Justin," she begged. "Please..." She tried to move her arms, but his strength on the belt's restraint was immovable. Her fingers closed on his shirt helplessly, bunched it in her damp hands.

He raised a brow, and his eyes were flame. "I love the feel of a woman's pussy contracting on me, so close, but not quite there, her arousal running down my testicles. I still haven't washed you off of me from last night, Sarah. Tell me you want me."

"I want you," she said, her voice rough. "Damn you." She made the leap, though the abyss had no bottom she could see. She didn't care. It was the leap she wanted, the soaring, the plunge. The bottom had become irrelevant.

Justin lifted his head, keeping the belt in place. His lips paused just over hers, those intent eyes so close.

"I want you, too, Sarah," he said. "I've never wanted a woman this way before. Ever. I need you."

There was a shift in his eyes, so quick she might not have caught it except she was trained to notice such shifts, even at a moment like this.

He *did* need her, desperately. Maybe it was just what happened earlier today, but somehow she knew he had a savage need to lose himself in this act with her. How often had she come home with that savage, desperate need, the need to dispel the pain and horror in an act of love and physical passion? She had settled for a civilized dinner and polite conversation about her husband's work and glossed over the details of hers, when what she really wanted was for him to violently sweep dishes and food to the floor and fuck her on the table with every ounce of his strength so she could scream and let all the blood and death be washed away on a flood of physical and emotional release.

"I need you, Justin. Now."

She had no warning. He dropped the belt, snaked his arm behind her, around the small of her back so her waist was cinched up against his body, and drove hard and deep into her at the same moment, using the power of his arm to hold her tight against him. The force of his movement shifted them, pushing them both against the window so she heard the frame creak ominously.

She imagined what it would be like for that window to pop free so her head, shoulders and breasts were bathed by the wind and sunshine while her thighs and pussy were clamped around him in the exotic shadows of his shop. Her hair fluttering free even as their thighs grew damp with exertion, friction and need.

Last night had been wild, primitive. This was primal. This was simple possession and escape, escape from a body in the woods, possession of a woman he appeared to want with an undeniable, raging hunger. She felt a matching need swell in her for him.

She dug her nails into his shoulders and groaned as he withdrew and surged back in, long full strokes that he alternated with a series of tiny movements. He drew out until she felt the ridges of his head tease her clit and the sensitive opening, then he drove in again, reigniting all her nerve endings. She couldn't breathe, couldn't even move, the power of the climax rising up into her like a paralysis where she had no energy to speak or struggle, just take all of him and pant for more. Each time she got close on those furious small strokes, he'd pull far out again, as if he were stoking a fire, seeing how hot he could make the embers before the whole thing burst into flame.

"Now, Sarah," he whispered in her ear. His fingers stroked her between her ass cheeks. She shrieked.

An earthquake began within her, all the plates moving, splitting open to show the fire raging at the center of her being and realigning whole continents of beliefs and conceptions. At the moment she was nothing but a new creation in his arms, the Goddess in the arms of the Consort, overwhelmed by his power and strength, the thrill of that connection deep inside her, the sense of completion.

It was both spiritual and blatantly physical at once, his grunts, her cries, the slap of flesh, her back rubbing against the rough wood of the dividers, a low, long moan as her climax shook her.

He spilled himself in her then, and she felt the surge of his seed rush along the contracting walls of her cunt. Long after the heaviest wave of the prolonged orgasm passed, she continued to shudder and jerk with the force of the aftershocks. She wrapped her arms more tightly around him, pressing her face to his neck.

The stillness of the room returned, punctuated only by their deep breathing. She should let go. In a moment shame and doubt would swamp her. Perhaps that was why she continued to hold on, thinking if she stayed in the circle of his arms, feeling his fingers tracing her spine, the flare of her hips, she could stave it off a little longer.

The screen door at the front of the store squeaked. "Justin?"

Sarah stiffened and would have scrambled away, but Justin tightened his arms around her. "Sshh, be still. Margaret?" He raised his voice. "Take the others and go on up to the classroom to change. I'll be up in just a minute. My partner for the night is changing in here."

"Oh, wonderful. All right." There was a murmur of voices, men and women both.

"It's all right." Justin slipped out of her and eased her down to her feet, holding her waist. "It's my Tantra class." He slid the other strap of the teddy off her shoulder and eased it down her body before she could organize her thoughts.

"What?" She made a futile grab at it, but he had it down to her ankles, and his broad back and shoulder were in her way.

"As beautiful as you are in this, I don't think you can wear it for the workshop. It would be distracting to say the least, and the thong and underwiring might constrict certain energy centers."

She was completely naked now, standing in the dying sunlight of the window. Herne straightened, his gaze caressing her as he tucked himself back into his underwear and refastened his trousers.

Before she could protest or ask the whereabouts of her clothes, he covered her mouth with his in a gentle but firm kiss, holding her naked body against his fully clothed one as he melted her fears, pooled them in the liquid heat in her lower belly.

"Justin." She struggled for orientation. "I'm dripping."

He smiled, reached behind him and tugged a soft towel off the screen. She extended her hand to take it from him, but instead let out a surprised noise as he insinuated his hand between her legs and began to clean her with soft rubs and pats, touching her thighs and her smooth folds.

"I can do it," she said, embarrassed.

"I know. But it's a pleasure to touch you, Sarah, and to take care of you. I was a bit rougher than I should have been."

"I liked that," she mumbled. Because she wasn't a coward, she looked up at his face. "You lost control. I liked that."

"I'll bet." A rueful smile touched his lips. "Now you know how it feels. I like it when you let go, too."

"Here." He pulled a robe from the screen, a soft satin creation of ivory, and threaded her arms through it. Some reality returned, and with it, a flutter of panic.

"Herne, I can't participate in some weird sex class you have. I'm a police chief."

"Weird sex class. A spiritual tradition that's over a thousand years old." He rolled his eyes, folded the fabric across her body and tied the sash. Justin held the ties wrapped around his knuckles to keep her from twisting away. "I have three couples in this class, Sarah. The women consist of a schoolteacher, a doctor and a housewife. I promise you, there is nothing about this workshop that will impugn your character in any way, and we will not be naked."

"So why am I wearing this?"

"Tonight, we're focusing on the woman, and I told all three of them to bring robes so they can stretch out comfortably and not be restricted in any way. Energy flow is important in Tantric practice. Tantra is, very basically, increasing the spiritual connection with your partner through erotic and intimate practices, and thereby increasing your closeness to whatever you call God."

"Using sex to get closer to God. I don't remember that from my Baptist Sunday school lessons."

He grinned. "It may be a little left of conservative, but it's not quite trucker massages in a trailer by the interstate either. Sarah." He let go of the robe ties, framed her face with both of his hands in a semi-impatient caress. "Trust me. I understand the importance of your job. I wouldn't endanger it."

Her jaw flexed under his touch. "You tricked me into this. Don't think I'm going to forget that."

"You can handcuff and beat me with your nightstick later."

"Smartass."

Chapter 8

ૹ

He was right about the composition of the class. They ranged from Margaret and Bill Robertson, parents of teenagers and dressed in casual conservative clothes that suggested middle-class America, to Dr. Erin Stouffer, who was aerobically toned, in her late forties, with a husband who wore his corporate business acumen as easily as his tan. The third couple was a pair of snowbirds down for the winter from Connecticut, and about to head back up in their sailboat before Florida began its sweltering summer. They were in their sixties, and the man sported a gray ponytail and twinkling eyes. His wife wore a soft nightshirt in tie-dye colors.

Justin moved smoothly into introductions and welcomed them all back to what Sarah learned was their second class. He shook every man's hand, and kissed each woman lightly on the mouth. He made genuine warmth look so easy that Sarah found herself enjoying being in his presence as much as the others did.

"Thank you all for coming," Justin said. "You all may be aware that Sarah is Lilesville's new police chief. She and I have only recently met, and I'm hoping we're beginning an intriguing and long-lived friendship. I coerced her into being my guinea pig for you tonight, so you'll be our chaperones to make sure I don't get out of hand and ruin my chances with her."

There was laughter and some speculative looks, but nothing unpleasant or affronted. So often, a cop learned to be polite and reassuring, but distant. It was best not to plan to get too close, because the potential friend could be involved in shit she didn't want to know about. It was easier to make friends with cops and their families, or other emergency personnel.

During her marriage, she'd become the silent arm appendage at hangouts with her ex's friends. There was no one to blame for that but herself. It was just hard for her to let down her guard. She was uncomfortably reminded that Justin had zeroed in on that about her right away.

Of course, he couldn't throw any stones. Justin offered warmth but still maintained his professional distance. He made everyone feel included and welcome without revealing the reserve. His quiet charm distracted them from seeing it. A cop had to make sure that reserve showed to keep his or her authority, but he was so clever at covering his she would have missed it, if she hadn't seen him when it had slipped.

But sex was one thing, real life was another. Who was Justin Herne? And what was the powerful thing that kept drawing the two of them together?

He gestured to the scattered cushions and rugs. "If you all will make yourselves comfortable on the floor, I'll prepare the area. Sarah, if you'll sit there." He pointed to one pile of cushions.

"Now, in our first class I explained the history and the philosophy. Tonight's about practical application. To start us off, I want to give you something to think about." He pressed the start button on a CD player and withdrew a long-stemmed match from a blue ceramic vase. He lit it with a silver scrolled lighter shaped like a dragon's head as the first strains of a relaxing percussion piece filled the room. "First rule. To have the type of sex you'll both enjoy, every time, it's got to be all about her. If anything ever goes wrong during sex, go back to Rule One."

There was laughter, some elbowing between the spouses. Justin moved around the room, lighting candles, and Sarah saw she wasn't the only woman intrigued by the elegant long fingers hovering above the tapers, just a hair from being burned.

"First, you create your sacred space." He gestured at the candles, nodded toward the CD player. "We prepare ourselves. Bathe, cleanse our bodies, dab on scents that we know will please our lover. This is your time, your sacred hour. Take the time. It will help her, but gentlemen, you will find you'll get the benefit of it as well. It's the difference between the steak dinner you choke down, versus the one you savor. You taste the juices in your mouth, enjoy it with good company, an attractive woman, a glass of wine, or a good beer.

"In this space," he waved his hand at their circle. "In this space, sex may or may not happen. The point is, you create a circle of intimacy in which anything can happen and likely will, because you are open to each other. There is no dissembling here, no shields. There may be some teasing." A smile flirted about his lips as he looked at Sarah. "But there is nothing in this circle except how you desire each other, in all ways. It works because your attention begins to center. All those peripheral spirals, work, cable schedule, kids, household chores, they are not allowed inside this inner circle. You step inside and you ward your space by whatever means necessary to keep all of that out."

He took a seat on a cushion in front of Sarah and motioned to the others to take the same posture with their partner. "Now, sit, knee to knee, and place your hand on your lover's heart. Not breasts," he warned, with a quick male grin that elicited snorts and some nervous chuckles. "That comes later. *Don't rush this.* This is the time you have together, just the two of you. It's a miracle. We all want to rush to that grand climax, but isn't the view most amazing from the greatest possible height? We'd never get there if we flung ourselves off that first available cliff ledge."

He positioned himself cross-legged in front of Sarah, his knees touching hers. She felt silly, but when she stole a glance at the other three couples, she saw they were looking at each other, so she relaxed somewhat. Justin took her right hand in his, raised it and placed it over his heart. He did the same with his right hand, sliding it under the loose neckline of her robe so the palm of his flesh met the skin between her collarbone and the beginning slope of her firm breast. He took her left hand loosely with his left hand, linked fingers and let their two hands lie that way between them, resting on the slope of his calf.

"Now, breathe. Deeply. Slowly." He raised his voice to instruct his students, but his gaze focused on Sarah's face. "Close your eyes. Don't strain to listen. Just open yourself to it. Become aware of each other's breathing, the thump of that heartbeat beneath your hand, that heartbeat that is yours, yours to cherish. The feel of the skin. The heat. Become aware of the circle of space around you, just for the two of you."

The candlelight flickered behind her closed lids, soothing her senses and narrowing her focus to the flesh and heart beneath her palm. Her self-consciousness began to recede as a tranquil stillness settled over the room. As he predicted, she began to feel Justin's heart, steadily thumping against her touch, a reciprocal caress. Her fingers moved lightly over his flesh, a tiny movement, as if she were stroking that life-sustaining center. Images drifted through her head. The wild coupling below, the urgency of his body driving between her spread thighs, the fire and intensity of his gaze only a breath from hers. His face bathed in moonlight from her bay window. His body wrapped around hers during that terrible, lonely hour of three in the morning.

As she felt her heart beat beneath his palm, she turned away from the demand that she feel guilt, shame, or doubt. She had never plunged into a relationship so immediately in all her life, and yet here she was. She didn't want to run. She wanted to have more, feel more, with him, but she needed to slow it down like this, get her feet back under her. Not to run, but to hold her own with him.

Heat vibrated from him, and it seemed to be settling around her body like a warm cloak. She was aware of him almost from the inside, every rise and fall of their breath bringing her deeper into herself, into him, as if they were sharing a consciousness. Despite the very recent coupling, she felt her breasts and womb stir, seeking a closer joining, as though it was the natural way of such an awareness, the desire to make a complete connection and fulfillment.

"You should all be feeling a quiet, strong sensual closeness to your mate now, a sense that no speaking is necessary." Justin's voice was barely a murmur. "You're relaxed, and yet you're also hyperaware of one another's bodies, and your attraction to one another, which includes as well as surpasses the flesh. Your attraction to the soul within, bound to your own.

"The steps we've taken, casting a circle and doing this breathing exercise, are good ways to start your journey toward lovemaking, but they are also good ways to reconnect, even if you don't have time for lovemaking. Just if you emotionally need to remind yourselves of your connection. It's not a bad way to settle down after an argument."

He left his hand where it was, but Sarah watched him study his students as they pulled their awareness from each other to focus on what he was saying. A smile touched his mouth at their obvious difficulty. "Sex is fun, sometimes over the top," he said, "but between lovers, it is always spiritual, a melding with the higher power that brought you together. Now, there are some variations on this that you might not want to do in mixed company."

He turned his attention back to Sarah. "The same breathing exercise. Start with the hands on the heart as we've done. But then do an equal amount of time with them on either side of the throat." He lifted his hands and laid them on either side of Sarah's slender neck, his thumbs caressing her jaw. She wondered if she'd lost her mind when she raised her chin to give him better access. His eyes heated, but he kept speaking in the same even tone without moving his touch from her throat.

"Then the breasts. Not to knead or stroke. Just hold them in your hands. Your wife can hold you here." He moved Sarah's hands so she curled her fingers over his biceps. "You can also do this breathing exercise while holding one another's genitals. Again, don't fondle or try to stimulate. You are simply cupping your hand over the area, heightening your awareness of those sexual centers and the power of touch." His lips curved. "You'll find that the more still you are, the more aroused you will get. If anyone remembers their science, they know that the denser the mass of electrons in a confined space, the more explosive the reaction will be when they finally get out to move freely."

There was some quiet laughter. Sarah saw spouses exchanging intimate touches, sexual but not inappropriate. The slide of Mr. Robertson's finger along the hem of his wife's robe on her thigh. Dr. Erin playing with her husband's chest hair in the open collar of his shirt, smiling at him. The snowbird couple squeezing hands.

"Now, we move onto the next exercise. You've gotten just a taste of the level of sensual connection you can achieve. You won't be able to feel it fully here tonight because we are in an instruction mode, and you'll want privacy to do it right, but you're getting the idea. Sarah, if you could lie back on the cushions, I'll show you some other things. Right, there you go, just recline, stretch out your legs."

He shifted so he sat behind her, with her between him and the rest of the class. "Rule Two, which relates back to Rule One. A woman doesn't turn on and off like a lamp."

He lifted Sarah's hand in gentle fingers and lifted it to his lips, brushing his mouth over her skin. He turned over her hand, and did the same to her palm.

Sarah stared at him, afraid to look at the other couples and let them see the need in her face that the simple caress evoked.

"You see her response?" He nodded, squeezing her hand and giving her a reassuring smile, though Sarah felt far from reassured. "A woman is a fire you build, and the heat, once ignited in this fashion, can last as long as you both could possibly want. Once you know this lesson, and know it well, you can keep her embers smoldering so the tinder strikes up to a blaze, igniting her again and again."

He looked around at his audience, and his attention stopped briefly on the doctor. "Most women need a great deal of preparation to relax fully and get the most out of sex. Most men as well. Just because a man can get it up and perform in zero to sixty seconds doesn't mean that he derives the maximum pleasure by doing it that way. Sex drugs have very little to do with physical handicap and everything to do with artificially stimulating the body to get you to the starting gate faster, because we perceive we don't have time to 'get ready' anymore. We choke our food down, rush sex, pump ourselves up with drugs to stave off everything from depression to natural anxiety and wonder why we're fat, unhappy, not satisfied with the sex we're getting and fighting all the time with our spouses."

At the uncomfortable glances exchanged, he nodded. "Yes, good sex requires us to take a hard look at our lives and how we're living them. That's why you make a sacred space.

"Now, Sarah is a perfect example." He motioned to her in her reclining pose. "As a police officer, Sarah needs even more relaxation time than most women, and most women need a lot." Chuckles. "You saw how she responded to that hand kiss. Most men will now make a mistake. She's softening. She's got that fluttery look." He spread his hands wide and bared his teeth. "Time to move in with both hands in grope position and your tongue out to devour her tonsils."

Sarah snorted with laughter, surprising herself. Justin paused to let the amused response of the others settle down as well, then dropped his hands and continued in a more serious tone. "She'll likely go along, but she'll be struggling to catch up, because you've rushed her. All you did with that hand kiss was touch a match to the wood. You've got to take the time to fan the flame, rather than shoving your skillet onto it and expecting to get something cooking right off."

He was astounding. As he continued with his suggestions, Sarah listened with half an ear, the other half of her simply listening to the sound of his voice and absorbing all the nuances of his presence close to her. He had the mesmerizing quality of a priest. That ability to soothe the psyche with the pitch of his voice, and his body language. A low volume sexuality enhanced the quality, gave him the credibility to take them all along and not worry about how it would look to a cynical outside world.

He turned his gaze back to her and Sarah's smile died at the potency of that expression. She was enjoying this. Enjoying being with him. Aching to be with him.

She was in trouble.

Chapter 9

☙

"I don't get it," she said. "You could be a CEO. You could be another Tony Robbins. Hell, you could be anything. Why run a little shop in the middle of nowhere?"

"You don't think what we did here tonight made a difference in their lives? An important difference?"

She sat cross-legged in her robe, watching him move around the room to douse candles and incense. She was more relaxed than she had thought possible, and intensely aware of him. Sarah enjoyed watching the way he moved, using a silver douser to put out each candle, checking the incense to be sure it had burned out fully. He had loosed his hair after the last person left, so for the first time she saw how it framed his handsome face, softening the gauntness, enhancing the curved lips and the dark eyes. His forearms revealed by the short sleeves of the black shirt looked strong and pleasing with their light mat of fine brown hairs. She could never get enough of looking at his long, capable hands.

Definitely in trouble.

"So you run this place because you believe in helping people to connect, and sex is a great avenue to it."

"You sound so incredulous." He turned off the overhead and left three candles lit, so they were wrapped in exotic sandalwood scent and candlelight. He came to join her, dropping to the cushions and lying on his side, one hand propped under his head as if he had all night to spend with her, though she expected he was as tired as she was. More, because he wasn't accustomed to starting his day with corpses. He closed his hand on her bare foot, warming her chilled toes with a gentle kneading.

"I'm just trying to understand."

"Okay." He inclined his head. "You've got part of it. The other part has even wider spiritual implications to me. Like what you saw last night in the forest. Sex done by a loving couple brings together the energies of the Lord and Lady for positive good, whether the couple is cognizant of the release of that energy or not."

She pursed her lips, considering. "I guess I can see that."

He arched a brow. "You don't seem uncomfortable with alternative faith topics, despite your Southern Baptist upbringing."

"Oh." She gave him a quick grin. "That's because I've got two influences. My parents were the Southern Baptists. My grandmother was Cherokee, very into the old ways. I spent my summers with her when I was growing up. Wicca's not much different at its core than shamanism." She looked down at him, at his hand working on her foot. She took a deep breath. "Thank you for tonight."

"Which part?" He shot her an innocent look, and she pushed at his shoulder.

"Creep." She fanned out her fingers on her knees, over ivory silk. "For inviting me to this class. My ex, he told me…well, the details don't matter, but I thought something was wrong with me. I couldn't heat up fast enough with him, and I guess I always thought it was me. I just wanted you to know that you're right, it does make a difference. It helps. You helped me tonight."

Why she was disturbing the garbage at the bottom of her psyche she did not know. She kept hoping it would decay and fade away into dust if she just left the shit alone. But less than thirty-six hours with Justin and she found herself rehashing the times she had spent with her ex-husband. She remembered the instances in the latter part of their marriage, when she had felt *maybe* interested in sex, interested enough to make it happen. He would start by massaging her breasts or rubbing her clit, and it made her feel mildly annoyed and itchy. If she concentrated hard enough she could get into it and make it happen for both of them, but he had been intuitive enough to know that sex wasn't her favorite thing anymore. Truth be told, most times she'd gotten more turned on by the prospect of a hot bath and a book.

This morning she had decided the night with Justin was a fluke, adrenaline and spontaneity combining. Hell, combusting. She'd convinced herself the ritual had somehow done a number on her subconscious. Those few minutes below, before the class had arrived, had destroyed the theory.

Lord, but he was a beautiful man to watch. His movements were elegant and yet entirely male, the way he had squatted by her just now, with that slight adjustment of his slacks, the drape of his hand over his knee, the long fingers artlessly drawing the eye. You could photograph any part of him.

Was it him? How could she be so unresponsive to her husband and so responsive to this man who was nearly a stranger?

"You're not what I wanted you to be, Herne."

"Most women don't know what they want, Sarah." His lips tugged up in a wry smile. "Most men, either, but women are far more complex creatures. The faces of creation move through you, and they are equal parts chaos and rhythm."

"No new age bullshit."

"It's actually old age bullshit. Lie back on the cushions."

His voice was soft, but the sudden intent focus in his eyes shot straight to her loins and clamored at her to obey without a second's thought. Her brain wanted to backhand her wimpy libido, but she settled for lashing out at Herne.

"How about you say 'please' for once?"

"Please, Sarah. Lie down upon the cushions for me."

She nodded, unfolded her legs. His hand went to her shoulder, easing her back. His firm grip reassured her, and the luxurious pile of cushions he arranged beneath her supported her back, shoulders, neck and legs so she felt she could lie forever in that position without discomfort.

"Good?" he asked, kneeling beside her, his face just above hers, the planes etched by light and shadow like the still perfection of a Greek Adonis. Or perhaps Osiris. Hades. Adonis seemed too innocent for what she saw in those dark eyes. She reached up and slid her fingers over his jaw, startling herself. He sat still for a moment, letting her touch him, then he turned his head. He pressed his cheek into her palm so her fingers covered his eye and touched his brow, as if he was drawing absolution from her touch. When he moved back, he took her hand, closing his fingers on her wrist. He took hold of her other wrist and slowly pulled both arms over her head and left them to drape decadently over the pillows. The position raised her upper body, tilted the angle of her breasts and pressed her hips more deeply into the pillows.

"He said I was a dead fish," she said abruptly. "In...in bed."

Justin paused, his body hovered over hers like the shelter of a dangerous guardian angel. When their eyes met, Sarah set her jaw. "I know he was mad when he said it. He wasn't cruel, normally."

"I'm glad to hear it."

He had been mad, but his words had scarred. She had learned that it took less than two seconds to spit out something that could never be taken back, like bullets ejecting from a gun. A life forever altered by the discharge.

"I guess," she said, thinking she was insane, bringing up something she had never talked about with anyone, "I wondered if it was true. No." She grimaced. "That's a lie. I believed it. Believe it. I guess I'm just thinking...maybe this was all just the spontaneity, the newness. But your class, it got me to thinking."

He folded his legs and sat next to her hip, bracketing her body with his own by bracing one arm across her. With his other hand he took the edge of her robe hem and began to draw it up.

"Justin—"

"Just to mid-thigh, Sarah."

He folded the soft cloth back to where he said he would, though a high mid-thigh, so she felt certain he was looking at her dampening pussy. Something in her stomach trembled, a knot of emotions and physical reaction that ached. Though she knew it was a warning she should heed, she lay still beneath his attentions.

"You have beautiful legs." He traced a path from inside the back of her knee up the inner slope of her right thigh. She swallowed hard as he went up, and up, to just beneath the hem, perhaps five inches from the area between her leg and the soft outer lips of her cunt. His fingers trailed down her leg to her knee again, an erratic path.

"What are you doing?" she asked, her question a bit breathless.

"Touching your leg." He tilted his head to fix one glittering eye upon her flushed face. "Just touching your leg."

"But it feels…" She caught her lip on a moan as he took the same path back up, the light pressure of his touch awakening nerves in places he was not even close to touching, like an erotic form of acupuncture.

"Surprisingly intense?" His lips curved, not in a smile, but something more potent, something that made her think of those lips on her flesh. "You're a very sensual woman, Sarah. But you don't believe that."

She managed to shake her head, and then her fingers gripped the pillows as his caress, now at the back of her other knee, shot a shudder through her body. Her leg lifted to give him better access, and her opposite knee shifted, widening the

107

spread of her thighs. His eyes grew darker, but still he did not move to touch her in a manner she considered intimate.

"As a cop, I'm sure you paid attention to the details tonight. And one thing you wouldn't have missed is how often I emphasized a woman's most important erogenous zone. Her mind."

He bent, pressed his lips to her thigh, the soft skin inside, but a full foot from the part of her that screamed for that moist touch. Sarah arched, gasping as he kept his mouth in that one spot, his tongue creating tiny spirals on the small area.

He straightened, his hand sliding down her calf, then reversing his track, his knuckles trailing back up the other leg.

"That's the part you had to close down to do your job, Sarah. He couldn't figure out how to make it open back up and you didn't know how to help him. So you both tried to make do by just stimulating your body."

Herne's voice was a murmur, so quiet amid the cacophony of sensations pounding her she could not rouse a defense against the analytical intrusion.

"I can do just this," he continued, "and it will bring you to climax. A woman's cunt responds to forces the woman herself does not understand, not consciously. That's why a man has to explore below the surface—" his finger dipped below the hem of her robe again, "—to pleasure her properly."

Sarah pressed her cheek into the pillows, bit down.

He spread out his fingers, used his palm and all his fingers to increase the strength behind his touch sliding up her leg, his thumb leading the way, a probing guide that stopped in the crease between pussy and hip. His other fingers curled, tightening on the flesh of her thigh, his smallest finger resting at the shallow valley between buttock and leg, a possessive grip.

He stopped there and Sarah lifted her cheek from the pillow. Justin took his time studying her, starting at her throat and working his way down, sliding his attention over her breasts, her stomach, still covered by the robe.

"What are you doing?"

"Sshhh," he said gently. "I don't need you to talk or worry about anything." He lifted his palm from her body, brought his hands to her face. He pressed fingers against her lips, teased them open, let her suck on his thumb, stroking her nose, cheek and jaw with his other digits. He slid his thumb from her mouth down her throat, down the neckline of the robe, and kept going when he reached the vee of it so the satin slid open in front of his path. When he reached the tie at the waist, he freed it and spread the garment open, so she lay naked under his gaze.

"All I could think about during the class was that you were naked under this, and how much I wanted to touch you. No." He pressed his fingers on her lips again. "Don't say anything. Let me just make love to you with words."

Phone sex in person, she thought, and wanted to say it, to ward herself with humor, but she didn't. She endured the cadre of butterflies moving about madly in her chest and stomach.

She nearly screamed in frustrated desire as he went back down to her legs again, and even further down, to the portion of the limb below the knee. His touch slid up her calf, starting at her ankle, just a slow, slow glide up her skin to the back of her knee, caressing the base of her thigh. He crossed over to her other knee, started down toward her other ankle, a triangle of sensation that seemed to focus the reaction of her entire body.

"My lightest touch here, this caress, makes your cunt get even wetter. Your breasts are aching. I can see the nipples getting longer, stiffer. Your thighs are open to me, without conscious thought, showing me your tender pink pussy, offering it to me. Yet it will be my simple touch here, no higher than your knee, that will make you come."

"Sure of yourself, are you?" Her voice could have been just the whisper of curtains at an open window, barely moving in a humid summer breeze.

"Sure of you, Sarah. Sure that despite your practical, trained mind, you can imagine what it would be like if I took off my clothes and lay down full upon you, my flesh against yours, my body between your thighs. You can imagine me holding you, you wrapped tightly in my arms, close to my thundering heart, as I slowly, slowly, push the head of my cock into your cunt. You're a tight fit, Sarah." He leaned in as his hand continued its idle glide from ankle to knee and back down again, another caress to the back of her knee, the arch of her foot. "Your pussy is so wet now, I can see the candlelight glisten off your moisture. I want to kiss you there, lick that arousal, take you into my mouth."

She sank further into the pillows, her body heavy with the weight of desire. Her breath was ragged, her hips and legs moving in a sinuous rhythm that matched the tidal flow of his fingertips against her skin.

"I like how your pussy pulls me in, Sarah. There's a moment of resistance when I think you're going to be too tight for me, then all of a sudden I'm sliding in, like a sword into a tight scabbard, oiled only for my blade. You haven't had anyone since you left your husband, that's why you're so snug. I like it. It's torture to pull almost all the way out, but the agony is worth it, something that feels so damn good I just have to do it over and over, feel those pussy lips suck on the head of my cock, like a long kiss. Before I know it, I'm slamming into you, seeing how much of me you can take."

She was gasping now, her hips rising to his words, no touch upon them but the heated air. The fingers stroking her legs felt like they were on her clit. The same movements he was making on the skin of her leg expertly manipulated that small inch of flesh that no man on earth seemed to know how to do exactly right. Or at least she hadn't thought so until this man did it without even touching the part in question. Justin

Herne would make Eric Clapton *and* Jeff Beck stop to hear his air guitar.

She felt every press, pinch and scrape against her legs deep in her pussy, and in her clit. Her breasts strained upward in sensual response.

"Ah, God, Sarah. You make my cock so hard. You make me want you so much." The hand drifted down her calf again, caressed her ankle, molded her foot. "I want to watch your pussy when you come. It ripples like the edge of a mermaid's tail, that graceful shimmering among the liquid...your liquid, Sarah. This time I'll clean your come with my tongue instead of giving a towel that pleasure."

"Justin—"

The orgasm roared over her and through her, bowing her up against the pillows. Justin's hand never let up on its slow glide on her right leg, dipping into the sensitive curve of knee and tracing the fragile bones, and it was the same as a relentless and perfect masturbation of her pussy, the heavy waves of climax pounding her though he touched nothing but her leg below the knee. Her fingers dug into the pillows, and she rode the sensation, her body rocking and her ears full of his passionate whispers, driving her on.

"That's it. Come for me. Come harder."

Her body at last slumped back, her limbs as weak as her first week of Academy training. She felt his hands still on her, touching quivering flesh, stroking, and then she gave a soft, keening cry. His lips pressed between her folds and he sucked the moisture away from shuddering flesh. He licked delicately as she jerked and convulsed in tiny movements under his relentless hold, crying out with every contact he made with her rippling cunt. He took his time cleaning her, putting his tongue deep in her, then polishing the swollen lips on the outside with sucking kisses and long strokes of his tongue. He did not neglect her thighs, washing the insides, that fragile network of bones between thigh and labia to remove the pool of perspiration and arousal that had gathered there.

"Now," he murmured. "Until you bathe, you'll feel that faint stickiness there, and remember my mouth on you, as well as your own climax. Dead fish, my ass."

He tied her robe, arranged it over her sensitive flesh, and then his face was there above hers, his dark eyes like rich fire. "Come home with me, Sarah. Please don't make me beg."

She never said yes, but she could not bring herself to say no. After a moment of silence, she made a noise of surprise as she felt his arms slide beneath her and lift her up. She had apparently dozed off.

"Okay," she said, her face against his neck, and then she didn't remember much else for awhile. The world narrowed to the flickering light of candles, and his mysterious eyes. "I can walk, Justin," she said as an afterthought.

"I know. Just let me take care of you."

Those seven words, every woman's dream, almost never translated into reality. For this floating moment, she decided to let it be true, to believe it wouldn't become a nightmare. She was vaguely aware of him carrying her outside, shifting her as he locked the store, sitting her in the plush seat of the BMW.

"My clothes—"

"I've got them. Don't worry."

Chapter 10

∽

The old Victorian home he lived in was in the small historic district of Lilesville, his aunt's home. She had driven by it yesterday once or twice, musing about the man who lived there.

The bedroom in which she woke was small, but the furnishings were antiques with the old wood smell that was comforting, familiar and classy. Gauze curtains fluttered at the open window, the screen permitting a breeze and the moonlight to illuminate her surroundings. A china washbasin and pitcher, an antique clothespress on which her clothes had been neatly hung. Her robe lay at the foot of the bed, on a folded white spread.

It didn't seem like a man's room. It was comfortable, and the tasteful choices reflected a reverence for things of enduring beauty, which was like him. However, it did not have the accoutrements of a man who slept there, like pocket change on the dresser. Perhaps his aunt's room. It did not have the vacant feel of a guest bedroom.

She remembered vaguely the warmth of his clothed body curled around her naked one, his hand stroking her hair, but she was alone now. Except at the Rite, she'd not yet seen him fully naked, but then his form had been a mix of shadows and fire. She would like the pleasure of seeing that body close up, though she did not deny the extreme eroticism of feeling his clothed body against her wholly bare flesh.

Had he worked some spell on her to keep her so relaxed and doubt-free? If so, it was wearing off some. Waking in a strange house and finding her life so neatly arranged around her was disconcerting, to say the least.

Sliding on the robe, she moved across the room and into the hallway. She heard the ticking of a clock and saw dim light coming through an archway at the end of it. Trailing her hand along the wall guided her way, and brought to her touch a variety of framed pictures the right size for photographs, likely a montage of past and present family.

The light was candlelight, of course. Did the man ever use electricity? A dozen pillar candles reflected against the windows of the sunroom, which served as a greenhouse for all the plants in there. There was a fountain and a lotus-shaped gazing pool, beside which was a carved bench. An altar created from the wide sanded surface of a large oak tree stump was graced by an arch of twisted branches. Twined in the arch and in a chain along the circumference of the altar's surface were the fresh white wildflowers growing all about Lilesville. Four more lit candles stood on the altar. It also held a wooden carving of a man-stag creature and a voluptuous Goddess, and four carved symbols burned into the compass points of the circle beside each of the candles. A tiny porcelain carousel like a child's music box made a triangle point between the figures representing the Lord and Lady.

Justin was in front of the altar, moonlight sliding down his bare pale body. His back was to her, just slightly turned so she could see his profile and the surface of the altar. He laid a flower at the base of the small Goddess statue, bowed his head to the Lord figure and then stretched his arms up. Gathering energy to him in a way she could feel through her skin, both as a woman and as an observer, he made a mysterious and yet intensely vulnerable figure. She had never really seen a man truly absorbed in prayer, in devotion for something larger than himself.

She stepped back. Even the intimacy of passionate sex did not give her the right to intrude on this. He turned his head and with a shock, Sarah saw tears in his eyes. He blinked them back quickly, and she pretended not to see.

"I'm sorry," she said softly. "I just came to find you."

Her gaze fell to his hand. He held a lock of hair in his fingers, the strand tied with a ribbon and a sprig of greenery. Watching her, he placed it on the altar, inside the chain of flowers. The color and texture was recognizable, since she had only handled it recently.

"You took her hair."

"A lock of it, yes."

She studied him a long minute. "I guess a lecture on how stupid that was wouldn't do any good."

"No." A faint smile lifted his mouth, but his eyes remained sad, distant.

Well, she had promised Eric she'd try to get more out of him. Since he'd barely given her time to breathe up until now, this was her first opening. She was veteran enough to take advantage of this opportunity, woman enough to feel a twinge of guilt for doing so. She acknowledged that she wanted to know more for herself as well and took a small step into the room.

"Am I intruding?"

"That's not possible." He went from his knees to his heels in one easy motion and shrugged into the cotton robe to the left of his feet. He turned toward her, belting it, and eased onto the bench. "Come sit with me."

She complied. His arm was along the back and it was a small bench, so she ended up under the crook of shoulder, with him gazing down into her face. It was as natural as the water pouring from the fountain to accept the kiss he pressed on her lips and drew out, his fingertips grazing her jaw. When he lifted his head, her hand lay on his knee, as if for balance.

Sarah cleared her throat, looked away. "The carousel. I don't understand that." She nodded at on the altar.

"It's...it's hard to lie to you, Sarah."

"Have you been?"

"No." His fingers tightened on her shoulder when she tensed and would have drawn back. "No. If I can't tell you something, I've simply told you I can't, or won't."

"Is it because I'm a cop you find it hard to lie to me?"

"No, it's not because you're a cop." His traced her cheek, that gentle touch that kept surprising her, as if he considered her delicate, something precious. It startled her to realize she had never been treated that way by any man in her life, and how much she welcomed it. The knuckle moved to touch her beneath her chin, his other fingers spreading out to feather her jaw. "It's not that at all," he murmured, gazing into her face with an expression of intent wonder that made her self-conscious, though not in an unpleasant way. She stifled the urge to speak or squirm beneath the regard that seemed almost reverent.

"I can tell you the truth about the carousel," he said finally. "I want to say I can't, but that would just be cowardice. The carousel is a small urn. It holds a handful of my daughter's ashes."

"Oh. *Oh.*" It was automatic, her hand closing over his on his knee, bare where the robe parted, her fingers firm and sure. "Justin, I'm so sorry."

He nodded, and now, when she saw him fight back the grief, she knew what had sculpted that gaunt, haunting quality of his face. She knew the psyche articles and the stress ratings, but most importantly, as a former homicide detective, she had seen the loss of a child crumble a person instantly, from the inside out. She wondered that anyone ever survived such a blow to the soul.

"I suppose I wanted you to know," he said. "Otherwise, I wouldn't have brought you here. Her pictures are all up in the hallway. I know she's at peace with angels somewhere, or maybe embracing a new life, a new incarnation someplace where she'll get a longer chance to experience what the world has to offer her. That is my faith, and that is what I believe. But I miss her, every day." He lifted a shoulder, shook his head and looked away at the moonlight playing in the fountain waters.

"Can I...do you want to tell me how it happened?"

That same half shrug, a slight gesture, like a wide range of movement might break him. Sarah moved in closer, laying her head on his shoulder. She wrapped her arm around his chest, curling her hand around his far side, thinking she could help protect his heart with the strength of her arm. His freed hand rose, touching her forearm. She heard the thud of his heartbeat. Slow, almost too slow, as if maintaining its normal resting rate was too much against so much pain.

"We were walking down the sidewalk together. Where I used to live. We'd take a walk each day. To the end of the street, turn the corner, walk up to the neighborhood store. The manager there was an older man who missed his grandchildren, so she was always welcome. We'd get a piece of candy for her, a paper and a soda for me, walk home. The road the convenience store was on was a busy one, but the sidewalk made it safe.

"It was over in a second," he said. "Maybe even less. She was holding my hand, laughing, looking up at me. A driver changing a CD in her car wasn't paying attention to what she was doing. She jumped the curb."

Sarah's grip on him tightened and he turned his face even further toward the window, so all she saw as she looked up at him was the strong straight line of his neck, the gray marble plane of his jaw and cheek, stark in the moonlight.

"The car didn't touch me. The grill rammed right into my little girl, threw her a hundred feet into the air. The car skidded by me, hit a tree. I can still feel her fingers in mine sometimes, that brief second before they were gone."

"Oh, Justin."

"She landed in traffic. On that busy four-lane road, not one of them hit her, even though she dropped in among them like a bird shot from the air. They all managed to stop in time, or were at the right place to miss her. I was running out even as she was coming down. I don't remember anything about the cars, even though someone said later I was almost hit by two of them.

"I thought, *maybe I can catch her*, only seconds before she landed. She...her head hit the pavement first. Then I was on the ground, holding her in my arms, and I knew. It was worse than dying, worse than any torture. She looked at me, blinked, those beautiful blue eyes, and I saw the light going out of them, it was so quick. 'Daddy, it hurts,' she said. And that was it. She died."

Sarah laid her hand against the side of his face, felt the tears there, and tasted her own at the corner of her mouth.

"They said it was a miracle she even had that second or two of life after she landed...that her brain function should have stopped immediately after such a blow."

"When...when did this happen?"

"Yesterday. A minute ago. Four years ago. It's all the same."

Eric thought Justin Herne had come to Lilesville to care for his aunt. Sarah realized the truth was more likely that he had come to Lilesville so his aunt could help care for him.

Justin bowed his head, his face still averted from her, but she saw his eyes close tightly, like his hand beneath hers on his leg. "If wishes were horses, beggars would ride." He lifted his head, looked at her. "We'd *all* ride."

She nodded. She understood that only too well, and knew he could see that she did. She wanted to ask about the child's mother, but he'd given her enough of his personal life for one night. As a cop she also knew how often the tragedy of losing a child was compounded by the divorce of the grieving parents, their pain and guilt so large it destroyed their love.

He let her wipe away his tears, then took her hand, brought it to his chest, held it. "You are kind," he said. "But, Sarah, I've a fine life. I don't want you to think I'm telling you this to distract you. I want you to investigate Lorraine's death as you feel appropriate."

Sarah studied his tired face, the handsome jaw and dark eyes that held so much. "But you still won't tell me all I need to know."

"You've already indicated you won't believe me, Sarah. I won't waste your time, or mine."

"If you believe she conjured something that killed her, you're right. It makes me question my sanity, being attracted to a guy who thinks 'the truth is out there'." She reached up and caressed his jaw. "But you might be as sexy as David Duchovny."

"Ah, flattery." He smiled then, and Sarah relaxed as the sorrow in his eyes receded.

He curled his fingers in her hair, tugging. "So, if I let you go tonight, are you going to be willing to see me again, or will we be back to 'Herne' and 'Chief Wylde' tomorrow?"

"I don't know." He'd been honest with her, so she gave him an honest answer. "I'd like some time to think, Justin. A little space. Let me come looking for you. One way or another, I promise I'll let you know how it's going to be. I won't make you guess."

"I'm not going anywhere," he said, though there was a forced lightness to his voice that suggested it was an effort for him not to push the point. Warmth curled in her stomach at the sound of it, a response to being wanted, desired. She laid her hand inside the collar of the robe, stroking the bare skin over his pectoral. "How long do you want?" he asked.

Her fingers found his nipple, threading through chest hair, and he caught her hand, stilling it. "Don't distract me," he said sternly, though she heard the humor in his voice.

"Okay," she said. She snaked her other hand beneath his robe and cupped the round curve of his testicles, accessible from the splayed position of his knees.

"Sarah." He caught both her hands, laughing then, and took her to the floor, pinning her body next to the gurgling fountain and the altar. "*How long*, or I swear I'll never let you out of this house."

"That's kidnapping, Herne." She grinned, and raised her legs, wrapping them around his hips. She pressed against his hardening cock, a sure sign she had dispelled his pain, something she recognized was more important to her than grilling him on the case, for the moment.

"A week," she said, staring up into his eyes as his touch caressed the rapid pulse in her trapped wrists. He lowered his head to stroke her throat with his tongue. "Give me a week."

Chapter 11

∞

A day was harder than she expected. Three days were unbearable. Even with the hundred things she was doing to help Chief Wassler with the investigation and the details of running her own town, the passions Herne had awakened in her body made her as physically stimulated as a teenager, coupled with the emotional agony of being hopelessly infatuated with the man.

Herne did cooperate with the investigation in other ways, helping to calm some of her concerns about his connection to the case. He gave Wassler the name of the woman who'd been priestess at their Beltane Rite on the night Lorraine Messenger was murdered.

At Eric's request, Sarah sat in with Wassler on the interview. Linda Egret was an engineer and middle manager at the county nuclear plant. The woman who showed up in dress slacks, soft lavender blouse and heels was far different from the naked priestess Sarah had seen. However, her green eyes were steady and compassionate, and she answered their questions and came up with a similar technical analysis of the ritual depicted in the crime scene photos. She did not dip her toe into the waters of what might have been called or how the woman had died, as Herne had. She had never met or heard of Lorraine Messenger.

Sarah passively listened to the interview between Eric and Linda Egret until that moment. "Mr. Herne didn't mention the woman had asked to be part of the coven?" she asked. "Wouldn't the two of you, as head priest and priestess, make those decisions together?"

"Perhaps." Linda hesitated. "But I trust Justin's judgment. He's never given me reason to doubt that he has the best interests of the coven at heart. He can be fairly arrogant about some things." A familiar smile touched her lips and Sarah was annoyed at the twinge of jealousy she felt. "But he sets aside his ego in matters of faith and the wellbeing of the group. He's a caring friend and a very spiritual man. That's what this is about, isn't it?" Her eyes darkened with anger as she studied the two impassive cops before her. "You suspect he's somehow involved in this. I can tell you that Justin Herne isn't violent, nor is he deceitful. He will do everything he can to help you solve this case."

"Miss Egret." Sarah leaned forward. "I was a witness to the Beltane ritual you performed with Mr. Herne earlier this week. I know you two are lovers."

Linda sat back, her gaze frosty. "You were on private property, Chief Wylde."

"Yes, I was," Sarah said calmly, though she was very aware of Eric's sudden attention on her. "Mr. Herne and I have already resolved the mistake. I apologize for invading your privacy. However, it occurs to me you may be withholding information because you have a lover's desire to protect him."

"No, I'm not. Justin Herne doesn't need protection. He didn't harm anyone. I know that as a friend and as a spiritual partner. We are not lovers, Chief Wylde. The sexual coupling of the Great Rite doesn't require that. It's most powerful when it is done by lovers, but it only requires two people comfortable enough with each other and themselves that they can lower their shields and permit the spirit of the Lord and Lady to come into them." Linda laced her fingers on the tabletop, met Sarah's hard gaze with a steely one of her own. "It is the Lord and Lady you saw come together to bless the Earth that night, not me and Justin Herne. Lovers are those who share heart, mind and soul, outside the circle as well as inside it. Justin and I do not share that bond."

* * * * *

It was a struggle to shift gears, going from three days of non-stop work on a murder investigation to a presentation at the Marion Middle School auditorium. Sarah sat backstage and looked over her program offered by a courteous teacher. The kids were getting a ninety-minute marathon on every social issue related to personal health. Family planning was right before her ten-minute bit on illegal drug use. She almost bit off her tongue when she read the presenter's name.

"Chief Sarah, this stalking of yours has got to stop." Justin slid down into the metal chair next to hers.

"You're the speaker on family planning?" She eyed him. "Do they know what kind of shop you run?"

"You, the moral barometer of the community, already told me I had a nice place," he pointed out. "So why are you shocked? Did you miss me?"

She had, every raging gland. "You really need to get over yourself, Herne."

"So you did. I've missed you, too." He settled back comfortably, stretched an arm along the top of her chair. He just hooked his fingers on the metal back, didn't even touch her, but his nearness made her skin itch. "How about you go to an erotic film festival with me tonight? It's just a five minute drive from here, far away from the disapproving stares you imagine would be on the faces of Lilesville citizens."

"Didn't I say a week?"

"Don't consider it a date. We'll even keep one seat between us, just like straight guys going to the movies together."

She had to tighten her lips against a smile. "Charm won't work on me, Herne."

"Mmmm. I'll keep that in mind. There's my cue. Now, where did I put that bag of complimentary hopping penises and discount coupons for my adult video selections?"

He rose, slipping easily into a professional manner with the teacher who came to escort him out on stage. Sarah shook her head. He was such an ass. And she was moving from lust and an as-yet-undefined emotional attachment into liking him. It was revolting and worrisome, because her gut wouldn't let up. She knew there was a connection between him and Lorraine Messenger, and that nothing could be more stupid than a cop who got into bed with someone connected to a murder. Her hormones and her heart couldn't care less.

She expected him to start with the basic building blocks of contraception, diseases, pregnancy. However, as with most things, he surprised her.

After his brief introduction, he pointed to a girl and boy sitting together in the third row of the auditorium. "I'd like you two to come up here with me, if you will."

There were the expected whistles and catcalls, and teachers hushing their assigned rows as the two teenagers reluctantly came on stage and he extracted their names from them. Mary and Travis. Mary was pretty in a quiet way. Not the cheerleader, but more of the nice girl that everyone liked. Travis was gangling and a bit pimpled, but had a beautiful head of chestnut hair and hazel eyes. Sarah wondered if anyone other than Mary noticed how handsome he was, or would be. Looking at him critically as a teenager would, she knew he was probably considered a geek, and Mary was a bit plump.

"Mary, Travis, how long have you been going together?" Justin asked. He didn't use the megaphone because he didn't need it. That sensual voice of his penetrated every corner of the auditorium as easily as it penetrated Sarah's defenses.

"Three months," Travis mumbled. Mary blushed.

"I knew they were dating," Justin explained to the audience, "because of their body language. They were sitting together in their seats, leaning so their arms were touching, from shoulder to elbow."

Justin smiled, waited for the jeers and oohs to settle down. "Physical contact is one of our most important ways of communicating with one another. Right now is an incredible time for all of you." He paused, looking out at them, creating a sense of intimacy with just one steady look, as if he were talking to each of them personally. Sarah leaned forward and saw even the teachers looked pulled into it.

"There will never be another time in your life when you will be so aware of the way someone's hand feels holding yours." Justin stepped behind the two, picked up Mary's hand, and placed it in Travis's. He closed their fingers around one another, turned them so they were facing each other instead of the watching audience. "Feels pretty good, doesn't it?"

The two kids grinned, embarrassed but unable to deny their feelings. Sarah found herself smiling.

Justin pointed a finger out into the audience, swept it across them all. "Someone's foot covering yours under the desk, that stolen kiss between classes. That very first kiss." He shook his head, took a deep breath and rolled his eyes, eliciting nervous laughter. "It's all so exciting, and yet it is the oldest ritual we know. The search for connection through touch, the desire to create a circle with a mate and become united. And because it is the oldest ritual, it is very natural to want that to progress to a complete physical union, a consummation of two bodies. What we call, clinically, sex."

He dropped his tone to a dramatic whisper and quirked his brow at them. The students reacted in appropriate teenage fashion. He moved back to Mary and Travis, put a hand on each shoulder while the students calmed back down.

His voice settled into that riveting cadence Sarah was beginning to recognize and enjoy far too much. It possessed a quality that conveyed something important and mysterious was about to be said and shared, and they would all be part of it, joined in its truth. He pulled something out that was inside of each of them, touching on a yearning that they each had, no matter its individual shape and form. Two hundred teenagers in an auditorium were as attentive to it as Laura Crittenden or members of a Tantra class. The night of the class she had likened it to the skill of a gifted priest, but it had been a comparison only. Now she acknowledged it. Justin *was* a priest.

"Sex is a never-ending adventure, the exploration of a lifetime between two people who love each other. You are no longer children, so it is normal for you to be thinking about it. There are many things you do not know yet, because you lack experience, but there are many things you do.

"Now, in a minute, I'm going to talk about the things you expect me to talk about. Protection, disease. How abstinence is an acceptable choice and the only surefire protection against pregnancy or disease. You'll need to think about those things, because each of you is responsible for your own actions."

He stopped again, nodded, and got some return nods from the students in the first few rows. "However, when you feel for somebody the way Mary and Travis feel about each other, it's like a huge shouting inside of your heart. The practical stuff hardly rises above a whisper in comparison. But contained within that shout of feelings is a very, very powerful force."

Justin turned to his two companions on stage. "Travis, if you and Mary were out one night, and some guy jumped you with a knife, you'd fight him to protect Mary, wouldn't you?"

Travis nodded, tightened his grip on Mary's hand. "You bet."

Mary showed her first spark. "And I'd help. I wouldn't let him hurt Travis."

Justin slanted a glance toward the wings and Sarah was immersed in warm and confusing feelings at the very brief look he sent her way.

"If this were six hundred years ago, Travis might be a knight of the Round Table, and Mary would be his chosen lady. She would tie her favor on his arm before he went into battle and pray for his safe return. He would fight any evil to protect her, to save her from a wizard or two."

Justin used his hands to good advantage, gesturing out at the audience in a subtle but dramatic manner that kept their attention.

"They would know then, as they know now, that the best part of each day is getting to be part of each other's lives, no matter what else they face. There's a lot to face out there, isn't there?"

When he got a wave of verbal assent, he nodded, his expression sober. "And we get to my point. The reality of what we face with each other day-to-day requires just as much heroism, even though it might not seem as dramatic." He returned his hands to the young shoulders of Mary and Travis. "Travis, you want to make Mary happy and protect her from harm, and she wants to do the same for you." His attention went outward again. "So I want you, all of you, to keep two things in mind when you think about whether or not you will have sex.

"First thing. Sacrificing your own immediate needs to protect a lover from a choice that can change both of your lives in unpleasant ways forever is as brave and admirable as jousting a dragon or saving someone from a mugger. You're old enough to know how to take care of each other. Protecting each other is an act of love, and courage. Never forget that, no matter what someone else tells you that you should do."

He stepped back. "You can sit down, Mary and Travis. Thank you." Justin watched them leave the stage hand in hand and return to their seats. Then he raised his serious gaze to encompass his audience again, focusing them with that aura of dramatic stillness that clung to his shoulders. "Now for the second thing.

"We can't dictate when and if you have sex." His glance went deliberately to Sarah, "But if you wait and do it with someone for whom you feel a strong emotional and spiritual connection, someone with whom you know love and forever might be possible, who has a respect and caring for you that surpasses their desire merely to claim your flesh, you will have a memory worth carrying for the rest of your life."

* * * * *

"So, how about the movie?" he asked, as they walked to the parking lot after the end of the program.

"Do they offer popcorn at erotic film festivals? Milk Duds?"

"Barbarian," he said, with affection. He laid an arm over her shoulders, his fingers caressing the skin on her arm. She slid away, self-conscious.

"I thought we said this wasn't a date. Seat between us, and all that."

A flash of temper crossed his face, but she saw him rein it in with difficulty. "So I did," he said. "But will you let me drive you there? It's not far, and we can come back for your car."

"I'll follow," she said.

He stopped by his vehicle and slid his left hand into his pocket. "Sarah," he said quietly. "I said I'd give you a week to consider where you want to go on this. But it doesn't sound like you're considering. It sounds like you're trying to build a wall as fast as you possibly can, so at the end of a week you'll be so solidly behind it that whatever is between us will be less than a memory."

How could she explain that her defensiveness came from the fact that he kicked away every foundation stone before she could barely plant one into the ground?

"How come you haven't asked about the status of the investigation? The real reason," she challenged him, before that smooth mask could settle over his expression.

"The real reason. Let's see." He pulled out his key fob, stabbed the unlock button so the car chirped at them. "There are three. One, I figured it was police business and you couldn't chat up the details with me, seeing as you think I'm involved. Two, I've already told you I know what killed her, but you aren't ready to talk about that. Three, when I see you, dead bodies are not what immediately comes to my mind. Unfortunately, it's apparently what comes to the forefront of yours."

He yanked open the door, slid behind the wheel. Sarah braced a hand against the hip side of her practical tailored black skirt. She had coordinated it with a gold blouse, over which she had worn her badge on a gold chain. She didn't like wearing a gun in a school, even though she knew the absence of the sidearm always disappointed the kids.

"So, I guess you're mad now and you don't want me to go with you to the movies."

Justin pressed his fingers to his eyelids as if he'd just developed a pounding headache. She tried to suppress the amusement in her face when he jerked his gaze back up to her.

"You're goading me."

"Giving it a shot." She shrugged. "You're too smooth, Herne. Makes me nervous, and it annoys the shit out of me."

"I know the feeling."

In a move she should have seen coming, he caught her wrist, yanked her forward so she tumbled across his lap. Sarah caught the soft fabric of the passenger seat and let out a yelp as he slapped her smartly on the ass three times and then spun her over in his arms so she was cradled in them on his thighs, the wheel pressing her in close to him. He did it so fast, she didn't have time to do much more than stare at him before he was kissing her, his hand holding her jaw, keeping her still as he plunged between her lips and took over.

Her bottom tingled from the none-too-gentle spanking, and it translated to a prickling sensation between her legs that his mouth stimulated with the dexterity of his tongue against hers. She couldn't think when he kissed her like this, so she held on and moaned softly into his mouth, clutching his shoulder with her free hand, her other pinned between her hip and his lower belly, her fingers latching onto his belt, hooking into his waistband.

She tasted his impatience and anger, and rather than raising the same reaction within her, it softened her, because she felt his need. Not just in the obvious place, pressing against her abused ass, but as an emotional hunger. While it was that need instead of the physical need that kept motivating her to retreat and spar with him, to hold him at bay until she could get control, it was perversely those same emotions that made her want to get closer. To enjoy feeling desired and cared for as she had at the beginning of her marriage, before it somehow had vanished, as if it had been an illusion all along.

She shoved at him and began to struggle, like a cat fighting its way out of a bathtub.

She was breathing hard, and his eyes coursed in deliberate appraisal over her tight nipples, down to her crotch where she knew as well as he did how wet she was. Then he lifted his attention to her face and let her see the intensity of those dark eyes, the desire to pull her into them, into his body, and immerse her in all the pleasures they promised. Her backside still stung, her lips were swollen, her breasts ached, and her thighs trembled. He had done it with three swats and one kiss. She suspected the man could kill her with actual sex.

Or worse, destroy her heart and mess up her senses so she had no radar left. Her radar had been damaged by her marriage and she hadn't figured out how to make repairs yet, though she'd been sure that getting involved with someone too soon was the wrong way to go about it.

He didn't let her scramble away. He lifted her in those lean arms that shouldn't be so strong and scooted her over into the passenger seat.

"We'll take my car," he said. "The theater's only a few miles away."

He started the engine and pulled out of the parking lot before she could think of anything intelligent to say, and then she didn't know what to say at all.

"So, how *is* the investigation going?"

She shot a glance at him, saw the smile flirting about his lips, and her tension eased.

"*Jerk.*"

He laughed, picked up her hand and kissed it, a quick brush of lips, then held it throughout the short trip.

She was content to let him do just that, and wondered at his ability to return them to an even balance with a few words, when he was equally adept at yanking the floor out from beneath her feet.

Chapter 12

ഇ

The film festival was being held in a restored 1950's movie house downtown. There was a glittering chandelier in the front lobby, illuminating a tapestry carpet and walls papered in rich reds and golds. The concession stand offered kettle corn as well as buttered, and a selection of old-time candies in clear glass containers with metal scoops to deposit one cup servings into small brown paper bags. Chocolate-coated raisins as big as grapes, maple nut clusters and Jordan Almonds all caught her eye, but it was the perfect cubes of chocolate-covered caramel she could imagine melting on her tongue even before Justin bought her a bagful. He waved away her money and got her a frosty fountain coke as well.

The ushers dressed in black tie formal wear escorted them into the theater. As they stepped down the aisle, Sarah felt Justin's hand at the small of her back, a gentle possession and protectiveness that her husband had never offered. As if because she was a woman who could protect herself physically she didn't need to feel protected emotionally by the warmth and strength of a man.

They were shown to two seats along the aisle, and the usher courteously encouraged them to make it known if anything interfered with their movie-going experience. The seats had deep red soft cushions, and the screen was covered by a heavy velvet curtain with gold tassels. Classical music mixed with familiar movie soundtrack scores played quietly over the hushed murmurings of other attendees. The theater was filling up rapidly, and as far as Sarah could tell, it was going to be a full house. Most in the audience were well-dressed pairings, coming in groups or as a single couple.

"It's crowded," she said.

"You sound surprised." He chuckled. "Sex is legal and it feels good, Sarah, to men and women. There aren't enough venues that make women feel comfortable to indulge their sensual curiosity. This is one of them. Ergo, a crowd."

"I guess." She settled next to Justin in the dim light. She immediately fished in the bag in his hand and took one of the caramels. "I haven't really been to any kind of movie in years."

"Why not?"

"Mmm…" She didn't answer right away, closing her eyes as the outer chocolate coating melted upon contact with her tongue. She bit down, mixing the flavor of the soft caramel with its lingering taste. "Oh, God. I might have found something better than sex." She cracked open a lid, grinned. "Almost."

"That's a relief. You don't like going to movies?"

"Well, I used to. It's just not like this anymore. It's rude people, cell phones, twenty advertisements instead of previews before the movie, dirty floors and worse bathrooms because the employees couldn't care less. I got tired of it, and stopped going. Thirty bucks to listen to some inconsiderate moron behind you talk about his tax returns to his buddies throughout the whole movie."

He nodded. "I discovered this place last year. They have to struggle to keep going, but it's always a pleasant experience. The ushers are here to make sure people don't act that way, so don't worry, you shouldn't have to draw your gun to keep people settled down. You can just enjoy the movie." He touched her chin with a finger. "And the company. I liked your talk on drugs. I plan to go home and throw away all my heroin and needles tonight."

She snorted. "Yeah, I can tell you're the type with railroad tracks up your arms. Glad to put you back on the straight and narrow."

"I'm glad you came tonight," he murmured.

"You didn't tell the usher to leave a seat between us."

"Well, it was crowded, and you couldn't reach the caramels."

"I could if you'd let me hold them," she retorted. "I'll make you go buy me another bag."

"I'll buy you ten more if you want." He smiled down at her. "Then hold your head while you throw them up."

She flushed, looked away. "You need to stop it."

"Stop what, Sarah? Enjoying you? Desiring to pleasure you, make you laugh? I like you, very much." He leaned closer, spoke with his nose pressed against her hair. "I desire you, I want you, I crave you like a drug. You didn't tell the kids what to do about that." The tip of his tongue touched the delicate skin just behind her outer ear and she shivered. "I don't think 'Just say no' is going to be a very effective method for me."

"Quit it."

"No. Every time I'm around you, I get lost. All I want is to plunge into you, be absorbed in you, drown in you." He caught her chin before she could pull away, and whispered the next words into the shell of her ear. "That's not a line, Sarah. No one's ever made me want to open myself up like that. I thought when I finally met her it would be a slow thing, some gradual attraction or friendship that would turn into something more. I saw you, and I got it all at once. The attraction, the lust, the need to know you, be your friend, earn your respect. It's damned unsettling, but I'll be damned if I'll let it become some high burn infatuation that will use up its fuel too fast. I want it to last, for a long, long time."

Now his fingers eased so she could pull back, stare up at him in the dim light provided by the brass wall sconces and overhead chandeliers. His countenance was alive with the emotions he had expressed, and they were drawing her in, like sirens calling her toward the rocks hidden in the pounding surf off a beach.

There was one free seat to her left. She got up, moved over, moved her coke over to that seat's cup holder. Justin watched her, his dark eyes like lagoons cloaked in the mysterious shadows of ancient trees. "What are you doing?"

"Making sure the fuel doesn't burn too fast," she said. "And retreating, a little bit."

"Because you want to, or because you're scared?"

"Because I'm scared." She couldn't be less than honest with him.

"Okay," he said after a moment, though she saw that tic of muscle along the line of his jaw. He settled back and held out his hand, his knuckles resting on the cushioned seat between them that was still warm from her body.

Sarah considered his open palm, the lines that creased the skin, the welcoming strength it offered. She laid her hand in his, felt his fingers close around it as the theater darkened and the curtain rolled back with a rhythmic clacking noise.

Justin leaned over, tugged her so she came close enough he could speak to her without disturbing the others. "This film is a montage of images and music, with storylines interspersed. It's about an inundation of the senses, not a plotline. It's supposed to be director Marie Gerault's finest erotic piece to date."

She felt a slight pressure against her leg and looked down. He was holding out the small bag of caramels, giving them to her to hold. Sarah positioned the bag between her thighs so she could use her one hand to dip in, and kept her other hand linked in the firm grasp of his on the seat between them.

He had on cologne tonight, the smell of a well-groomed man, a man who had taken care to be pleasing to her. With that and his two tickets, it was obvious he had known she'd taken Eric's place on the speakers' list. She drew a deep breath and let that thought and those scents fill her. The first strains of the film score began.

The name of the director had not meant anything to her, but she soon understood Justin's appreciation.

The first shot was a close up of an orchid. The camera zoomed in, followed the line of one petal, lingered on a glistening drop of dew barely holding onto the delicate edge of the white, veined curve.

A hand came into the frame, a male fingertip tracing those crevices, gently pushing into the folds to stroke the texture deeper within. There was a soft woman's sigh, and wind ruffled through the petals. The image faded and evolved, a seamless transition from the stroking of the exotic bloom to the stroking of a woman's clitoris and labia. The shot widened, and her thighs were strewn with the orchid petals. Drops of dew were still on them. The male finger touched one of the petals, gathered up the moisture and feathered it across the clitoris. He picked up a petal, shaped the silken fabric of it over the clit's shape.

The profile of the man's face, the long sloping line of his jaw, came into view. Slowly, slowly, his tongue inserted itself into the vaginal folds beneath the hooded clit. The woman's breath rasped, and the music became all winds, underlined by a slow drumbeat that thrummed in Sarah's chest even as she shifted, aware of the arousal growing in her own cunt, watching the woman's being so beautifully tormented.

The camera pulled back so the audience could now see the woman from waist to mid-thigh, and the full profile of the man's head. His dark wing of hair, his shaven jaw. His hand fanned out on her thigh, slid under it and rolled her to her side, so now they saw a lovely heart-shaped ass, two petals clinging to one cheek. He rolled her all the way over to her stomach, scooped up a handful of ivory and burgundy petals and scattered them so they fluttered down onto her buttocks, the flesh quivering at the light contact.

Justin's fingers had begun a slow, idle stroke down the center of Sarah's palm, and now he made a lazy circle at her wrist, caressing the pulse jumping there. His hand was warm, his grip gentle but strong, and the yearning between her legs tightened, making her legs twitch.

The man's long fingers followed the crevice between the woman's cheeks, guiding the petals so they lay there in a line, teasing the sensitive area. The woman's hips were moving, small circles, her thighs spreading for him. She whispered to him, the words unintelligible, although the need was not. Sarah swallowed as one finger dipped, guiding a petal deeper between the cleft, using it to massage her anus hidden within that fold. The other petals tumbled down to the valley where her thighs and the curves of her bottom met.

The beat picked up, became more primitive, as both his hands entered the scene. He parted her thighs wide, the petals drifting to the ivory satin sheets beneath her body. The woman whose face they could not see, so that she became every woman watching, moaned, and the soundtrack somehow echoed and enhanced it, vibrating the desire through all the watching bodies.

The hand lifted, that strong hand with long fingers, and then came down in a firm slap. Sarah jumped. The blow left a red handprint on milk-white skin. Another blow, then another, and Sarah remembered Justin's fierce, short spanking, and how it had stirred her in a way she did not anticipate, as this was doing.

She wanted him. Now. This second, or her lower body was going to utter a vocal scream of need.

Was everyone else as affected by the film, or just those who had recently rediscovered their hormones? She stole a glance around. The audience looked as absorbed in the film as she was. Civilized behavior dictated that they disguise their full response, but she saw enough parted and moistened lips and crossed legs to think that others were feeling the same pounding in between their thighs, matching the rhythm of the erotic music.

The spanking was over, and the hand smoothed over the curve of the rosy buttock. Using the nail just a bit to leave a light scrape, the man traced the crease between the weight of the cheek and the top of the thigh. The woman sighed, the sound captured and embraced by the wind as part of the music, and then the camera shot moved back in, focusing on the flesh of his hand, examining the beauty of the knuckles, that ability to curl, bend fingers to touch, press, stroke. When the view widened again, the scene had changed. The hand was pressed against the bare abdomen of a woman dressed in a sheer tight top sprinkled with sequins, and harem pants slashed up the side so as she turned, the flank and thigh were exposed, as well as a hint of the soft pelt of hair covering her mound.

An unsmiling sheik, his face indiscernible in shadows, let her go. She began to dance for him, a sensual belly dance where each leg turn and undulation brought a gift, the swell of her breast against the binding of the top, the sheen of sweat on the small of her back, the fluttering of the diaphanous cloth over her ass as she turned.

The shadows shifted, and the audience could see the intense dark eyes of the man who watched her every move. He lounged back on a pile of cushions now. As he wore nothing but an open silk robe over loose pants, it was possible to see the increased rate of his breathing from the rise and fall of his smooth chest, and the growth of his erection against the pants as she danced.

She loosed her hair, and it spun around her like a velvet cape, then out. Her arms did a dance of their own as she came to stand between his knees and dance for him, her eyes large, round, liquid, her lips parted, tongue touching her teeth.

He reached up, tore the sheer gauze of her top away so her breasts were loose. She did not break the rhythm of the dance, continuing her rolls and twists and shimmies. Her pert nipples grew erect from the movement of her full round breasts, responding to her own sensual display of them.

It was Valentino's Arabian Nights, only technology and movie effects made it real, with the music score and the fluttering of the tent cloth. They captured the bead of sweat at her jawline, closed in on it, followed its slide down her throat, its trickle to the top of her breast. The sheik's hand came into the screen to cover that drop, cup her breast and weigh it in his palm. His thumb rubbed the perspiration into the areola. Soft Arabic whispers joined the music, and Sarah did not need to know the words to know they were murmurs of passion, heated promises, oaths of devotion.

The film was supposed to be ninety minutes, and each subsequent scene started with that male hand and finished with it.

Sarah was a disciplined person, so she made herself sit through every image, her heart racing or slowing with the mood of each scene as Justin's hand continued to caress hers. He stroked the delicate veins of her wrists, traced and captured each finger, dipped into each curve between. At forty-five minutes, halfway through the film, her body was damp, coated with a light sheen of perspiration like the harem dancer, and her pussy throbbed so hard it was painful. She had never wanted to touch herself so much, or have a man touch her. She became more and more still throughout the movie, except for intense, spasmodic vibrations in her limbs she could not control, a trembling that she knew Justin must feel through his contact with her hand. She felt his eyes on her, watching her, and when his hand slid down her arm, just an inch or two further than her wrist, she gasped at the new ripple of sensation.

She didn't want a quick mechanical rush of release, a simple application of friction. She wanted to be joined with him again, filled by him, feel that rush stroking her tissues within and without, feel the weight of his body in her arms. She wanted all of it, the whole experience, and she wanted it now. And forever.

She was losing control. Was she losing her heart to this man or was it just lust? She felt bound to him in a way she did not understand at all. It was physical desire, but it was also pure, bone-deep attraction. He interested her on a tremendous number of levels.

She needed...oh, hell, she *needed*, period, and she wasn't going to analyze the hell out of it. Sarah bolted out of the seat, tripping over his long legs to get past him. "I've got to go," she rasped, and fled up the aisle.

She burst out the exit door, into the side alleyway where movie patrons were funneled at the end of the movie. The detail-oriented owners had not missed an opportunity, mounting a display of movie posters out along the facing brick building and arranging the alleyway into a courtyard of sorts, with cobblestones and a wish fountain into which patrons could throw their change and play with the Japanese koi swimming there. An old bicycle had been turned into a decoration, petunias spilling out of its basket and impatiens gathered in pots around the wheels. It leaned against an old-fashioned street lamp, wrought iron with a trio of glass globes. Chimes hung from the decorative curls beneath the globes and toned softly in the warm evening breeze funneling down the isolated alleyway.

Justin came out the door behind her, but she backed away from him, circling the fountain to keep something between them. "No, don't touch me. I'm going out of my mind." She paced. "I'm not like this. What are you doing to me?"

"I could ask the same of you. Do you think it's ever been like this for me, Sarah? Maybe you just like me. Maybe I just like you. Why is our attraction so difficult for you to accept? Haven't you ever been drawn to someone?"

"Not like this. Not this all consuming, *everything* feeling. I don't know what I feel for you, because you've got me all revved up all the time, with your movies, and your Tantra, and your shop. I'm out of my depth, and you're taking advantage of it. I'm confused—"

"Now look." He closed the distance between them and swung her around, his eyes and mouth hard. "I haven't taken advantage of you. I told you. It's never been like this for me, either."

"I don't know that. I can only speak for me. You've got me all confused, and I can't think past the lust right now to know how I feel for you."

"Then let's get the lust out of the way."

He caught her wrists and yanked her into the shadows at the back of the courtyard where a small container garden was clustered in the corner. She caught the fragrance of lilies before he had her up against the brick.

She expected violence and roughness, the release of the storm of energy vibrating from him. However, instead of crashing it over her like a wave, he stopped. Simply held her body against the wall, making her stare into his face, feel her own need bouncing against his like electrons in too close a space, as he had said. She whimpered as he leaned in at last and pressed against her from chest to knee. He cupped her jaw in his hand, rubbed his thumb down her jugular, and his knee pressed against the seam of her thighs.

"Open for me, Sarah," he said, a soft command she could not deny.

She parted her thighs and moaned as his hard cock pressed against her clit. His hand worked under her skirt as he studied her face, his own intent and a little frightening in its determination. He caught the crotch of her panties in his fingers and Sarah gasped as he tore them with one yank, making her stumble forward into his body. He caught her by the waist and turned her so the controlled fall continued. He took her down to the soft patch of edged turf grass they had put in around the small garden.

There, at last, she got what she had wanted to feel, his body covering hers, his hips between her legs, the weight of his chest on hers. He captured her face in both hands. "If you want me, Sarah, unfasten my trousers. Put my cock in you. Make us one."

Her fingers moved, and he lifted just enough so she could slide his belt free and make her fumbling fingers do as they both wanted. She opened his clothing and reached for him. He filled the curl of her hand with an impressive solidity that increased the reaction between her thighs, her pussy preparing for him.

There he was, powerful and full in her hand, hot, pulsing, alive and rigid with wanting her. *Her.* Linda Egret's words flashed through her mind. *Lovers are those who share heart, mind and soul, outside the circle as well as inside it.* What she held in her hand was part of the evidence, but even stronger was what she saw in his eyes as she touched him, and felt in his heart, thundering against hers.

"Now, Sarah," he whispered, his teeth showing, his hands clutched hard in her hair. "Please. Take me in."

She lifted her thighs higher and guided him to her warm and slick gateway. He passed from the grip of her fingers into the grip of her pussy, that fist of muscle that he had to push through, heightening the sensations for them both at the tight fit. He thrust all the way home, seating himself deep inside her, two sacred elements of a temple joining to form something that might last thousands of years.

She shuddered, moving her hands to his shoulders as he began to pump into her. Once, twice, and the images of the screen, the heat of his skin and the friction of his cock against her aroused flesh conflagrated and erupted. Unbelievably, she was climaxing, sinking her teeth into his shoulder, feeling his grip on her waist and hip as he pounded into her, moving them backward on the grass.

He groaned against her temple, his fingers flexing on her in that way that told her he was getting close to his own release. She tightened her grip within and without, stroking his cock with muscles she didn't know she had. The wonder of female power swept over her as she watched him lose control, grunt her name because he had no voice or mind for polish, and she held onto him, held him to her as he spilled into her, sending a flood of spasms along her channel that made her whimper softly in return and tighten her embrace around his shoulders. She reveled in the sensation of his hips pumping, sliding against the inside of her thighs, his slick buttocks bumping against her heels as he finished, emptying all of himself into her eager womb.

Sarah closed her eyes and just held him a moment, listened to his breath against her ear and felt his fingers stroking her waist, the side of her neck as he propped his weight on one elbow, but left his cheek against her forehead.

"I love the way you smell." She knew they should get up and get dressed, but she didn't want to do so yet.

"Oh." His lips pressed the corner of her mouth. "And how's that?"

"Male. The incense in your shop, the antiques in your house, the vanilla candles. The smell of you on my thighs." She opened her eyes and gazed into his face, just above hers.

"So, now that you're not all 'revved up', Chief," he teased in a murmur, though his expression was serious, questioning, picking up the thread of tension that had begun this moment. "How do you feel about me?"

"I want you to take me to dinner."

"After all those caramels?" His eyes crinkled with humor, underscoring what a handsome man he was. Her vagina contracted on him, and his eyes heated. He pressed a fervent kiss to the side of her lips, touching that corner with his tongue, a light flick.

"Which melted in the bag," she retorted, nuzzling his jaw. "Uneaten, and left behind. No, that's not what I meant. Not now. I don't..." She closed her eyes, shook her head to clear her sex-fuddled brain.

"I need that week, Justin, as I said. "She touched his lips before he could speak. " And then I need you to take me to dinner. A normal date. No erotic films, no Tantra classes, just you and me." It was awkward, but she was going to say it, partially because she trusted him enough with her feelings to say it. "I've never experienced anything, physically, like you. It's overwhelming."

"My ego would be inflating, if I didn't hear a 'but' coming." He propped his second elbow on the other side of her face so it was caged there and she could not hide from him.

"But…" a smile crossed her face as he shot her an I-told-you-so glance. "…I need to know if there's more here than that. I'm not a fuck' em and leave' em kind of girl. I never have been. If this is going to keep going, I have to know it's real. Okay?"

"What do you think the chances of that are?"

She stared up into his dark eyes and felt nervous, vulnerable. "What do you think?"

He placed a kiss on the tip of her nose, then put his forehead against hers. "Chances of that are very, very good. Now I think I better get up before the movie lets out and the police chief of Lilesville is seen with some bare-assed guy on top of her in an alleyway."

She shuddered. "It sounds so sordid when you put it that way."

He rose to his knees and rearranged his clothing, then gently slid the hem of her skirt back down to her knees, his hands caressing and strong. "It's not sordid in my mind. Nothing I've done with you has felt that way." He fished in his pocket, came up with her scrap of underwear and a linen handkerchief. He offered her the kerchief to clean herself and studied the panties. "I believe I owe you some lingerie."

"No thongs."

"Spoilsport." He chuckled. "I do have at least one pair in the shop with full coverage." He helped her up. "Of course, they're crotchless."

She reached to snatch her panties from him but he held them above her head, made her jump for them until she stomped on his instep and recovered them neatly. He used the advantage to pull her into his embrace.

Instead of the kiss she expected, she found herself drawn into a close warm hug, her face nestled against his chest. Her arms crept up his back and she held on, just held on in the moonlight. As he laid his cheek on the top of her head, the fountain gurgled quietly behind them. At least for this perfect moment, she knew she needed nothing more than that, and his embrace, to be at peace.

Chapter 13

ဢ

He hadn't taken her right home but to an ice cream shop, where they'd shared a sundae and her knees fit between his beneath the small table. They talked about the movie, his aunt, how he got started in retail, her Academy training and family. It was a hint of what he knew she wanted with her request for a normal dinner, and he wanted to get a head start on it, give her something to think about other than the sex for the rest of their week apart.

He liked talking to her, listening to her. She obviously felt the same, and he could tell those feelings weren't surprising her as much as they had at first. It was very comfortable and sweet to hold her hand on the table while they dipped into the same bowl of ice cream. While he knew it might be a mistake, he couldn't help but ask about Chicago.

"Eric told me you saw some pretty heavy things in your previous job. Is that why you're here?"

"No." She shrugged. "The job is the job. It gets bad, but you're there to stop the bad guys." She put down her spoon. "It's when you're ambushed from the inside that it falls apart. That's really why I needed a break. My divorce happened right after the worst bust of my career, and the two fed off each other. I suppose Eric told you about the bust."

"No. I looked it up."

At her surprised look, he laid his other hand over her free one. "I told you, I'm interested in you, Sarah. Those two bullet wounds had a story to them. I got the paper version."

"Overly dramatic." Her fleeting, haunted expression told him that, if anything, the article had understated it. He didn't dredge it up further for the woman who had lived it. One, because she had answered the question he had wanted answered, and two, because he remembered every word of the article.

A drug bust strategized for months, nine cops going in, his Sarah one of them. Finding out their inside source had set them up, they faced down a gang of ten with AK-47's and armor-piercing bullets. When it was over, only one person was left standing to pull a trigger, and that was how they determined who had "won" the engagement.

According to the article, that last officer, name withheld by request, had pulled herself to her feet, one bullet already lodged in her abdomen, no more than an inch away from her spine. She stumbled across fifty feet of a warehouse floor littered with bodies, calling out to the last conscious drug dealer to give up as he fumbled to reload a spare thirty-eight in the front seat of his shot-up car. She fell, dragged herself forward on her hands and knees. He cocked the weapon at the same moment she reached the car door and pulled herself up. She put a bullet in his face, and he fired his weapon into her kidney. She only had one now. Four officers killed, six drug dealers dead, the rest critically wounded. She collapsed, still holding onto the door with one hand, and that's how she was found, a scene that the papers had likened to something out of Baghdad. Four officers killed, six drug dealers dead, the rest critically wounded.

His fingers tightened over hers. "You're a warrior. A very brave woman. Whatever the reason is that brought you here, I'm glad for it. If I could have spared you a moment of fear or pain, I would. But I'll gladly be here if you need me to soothe your dreams and give you better ones."

"You already are." A flush rising in her cheeks. "My turn. I want to ask you a question now."

"Anything."

"Did you ever...were you ever married, or did you live with someone?"

"Just my little girl. There's been the occasional woman, but they didn't stick."

"Maybe it's your approach, breaking into their houses and all."

"I actually went to seduce Chief Owens that night. I forgot he had retired and you had moved in."

"He didn't even live there."

"Ah. Must have forgotten that."

She struggled against the smile and lost. "If you're this much of a smartass all the time, no wonder women don't want to hang around to cuddle."

"Despite my godlike status, Chief Sarah, I assure you I fall into a post-coital coma just like all men. I am oblivious to cuddling, or the lack thereof."

She knew he was lying. "Will you call me just by my name, please?"

Her tone was soft and Justin looked up, surprise crossing his handsome face. "Sarah," he murmured, his gaze holding hers across the table.

So he had never known it, that intimacy of living with someone, but she sensed now that he longed for it. He longed to be consort to a woman in fact, as he was to the Goddess in his faith. Having a child, then losing her, would have taught him the value of intimate bonds. She knew losing the love of her husband had taught it to her.

There was a jukebox in the ice cream shop, and Elvis crooned about the futile advice of wise men not to rush into things. He knew he couldn't stop himself from falling in love. Sarah felt the slide herself as Justin heard the music, and a warmth stole into his eyes. He rose, drew her to her feet.

"Justin, this is an ice cream shop."

"And there's just you and me and one teenager writing an English paper. Come here."

He brought her into the circle of his arms, and she felt it again, that sense of his strength and protection, freely offered to her as if it was something she could lean on, draw upon as needed. She put her hand on his shoulder, and his slid around her waist. Sarah caught the teenager's sidelong look at them before she rested her temple against Justin's neck and closed her eyes, just letting the music sink into her, that velvet golden voice, the feel of Justin's arms, the smell of ice cream.

As they danced, his hand eased down to that shallow and delicate curve of back over the flare of her hips. He hooked into the waistband of her skirt, his fingers spread over her hipbone, his thumb tracing her skin just above where the swell of her buttock began. As they continued to sway and turn, his thigh eased between hers and she found herself leaning into his weight, so each shift of hips rubbed his thigh against her mons and tissues that were starting to throb with the friction. His arms held her close, and she knew she should pull away. What they were doing was not visibly immodest, but still, if someone looked close, they would know.

"Relax." He pressed his hand against her back. "Lean on me. We're just dancing."

She was doing more than dancing. She was falling, tumbling, and he was there, waiting to catch her in open arms.

* * * * *

When she woke Monday morning, Sarah's feelings about Justin Herne were not uneasy. He had left her at her door Friday night with a brain-numbing kiss, but he was giving her space and romance, and she was starting to feel like she could relax and enjoy what was happening between them. They'd scheduled their dinner date for tonight.

"Chief." Dexter met her at her office door. His expression wiped the easy smile of greeting off of hers.

"What have you got?" She opened her office and tossed her key on her desk.

"They ran the search on Lorraine Messenger through the Gainesville system for Chief Wassler, like you said. She came from Richmond, Virginia. She's pretty much worked, hooked or did small dealer work to feed her habit through several states. She was caught a couple times, but the stuff was too minor to hold onto her. A social services report was made on her when she was hospitalized once in North Carolina."

"Why was social services involved in an OD?"

"It wasn't for that." He paused. "This just sucks out loud, Chief. Everyone likes Justin Herne."

Sarah halted the process of hanging her gun harness on her chair and turned slowly, ice freezing her bagel and coffee breakfast in her gut. "What does Herne have to do with it?"

Dexter extended the copies in his hand to her unhappily.

"She had a baby in the North Carolina hospital. Justin Matthias Herne is listed as the father. He took custody of the child with her written consent. She hooked her way back up to New York, and I don't find any connection between their living arrangements until three months ago, when she drifted into our area."

"And wound up dead." Sarah picked up her keys, slid the gun belt back over her shoulder.

"Chief Wassler's in a staff meeting this morning with Marion City Council, so they haven't acted yet, but Lieutenant Ford thought you'd want to know."

"Yeah. Call him, tell him I'll go get Herne and bring him in to them, since he's in our jurisdiction."

"Are you sure, Chief? Maybe one of us…if he's dangerous…"

"Trust me, Dexter. Compared to me at this moment, Justin Herne is as dangerous as the Easter bunny."

* * * * *

She was enraged. She was shocked. She was hurt so deeply she couldn't face it. It felt as bad as her husband's betrayal, but that didn't make sense. There was no way Herne could have gotten to her heart quick enough to hurt her like that, so she had to conclude that the previous hurt had simply amplified this one beyond realistic proportions.

Still, this betrayal had a unique, searing quality all its own. She turned away from the pain, focused on the rage, but then realized she couldn't lead with her emotions. She forced it away from her mind as she pulled into the driveway at his house, willed her heart and mind to become a single, automated unit, incapable of operating on any frequency but pure, hard objectivity.

But it was not objectivity that made her try the door and enter without knocking when she found it open. The BMW was out front and he had told her the shop was closed on Mondays, so she knew he was there. The irony of it was not lost on her, considering their first meeting. The entranceway had an ornate hallway tree that was probably two hundred years old, and the cherry wood gleamed with care and attention, like all the things he possessed. She hung her coat on it, left her shoulder holster on.

She didn't call his name. She wanted to find him wherever he was. She went up the hall, past pictures of a laughing little girl and his aunt, other family members she did not know.

As she stepped into the sitting room, she didn't allow herself to feel, just studied her surroundings in the light of day for the first time, painfully aware that thought might apply to their whole relationship.

The couch, sitting chair and recliner clustered comfortably around the entertainment center. A pair of men's shoes had been kicked off under the coffee table, and there was an afghan thrown over the arm of the sitting chair. Today's newspaper rested on the side table next to the recliner. All the little details of his day-to-day life she had wanted to learn about him, in the same way they had shared the sundae. Savoring each bite.

A roll top desk, chair and side table formed an office nook, and the surfaces of the furniture were stacked with books and papers, an ongoing project. She moved to it, and when she reached out to draw one of the open books to her, she brushed the mouse. The screensaver dissolved, revealing the picture on the screen, and it jerked her attention away from the content of the open book.

The wraith-like creature depicted had fangs and very erect genitalia. Its appearance disturbed her, for though its attributes warred visibly between human and not-human, its humanity was undeniably enticing, seductive. Its red eyes burned into her. Sarah stepped around the desk to read the text of the article in which the creature's picture was embedded.

Incubi are the male counterpart of the succubi. A class of demon, they disguise themselves as human women or succubi, copulate with unsuspecting men, and then take the procured seed and use it when they seduce women. An incubus is sterile, incapable of producing an ejaculation of its own seed. While overpoweringly seductive, it is said that the incubus can choose to make sexual penetration a very painful experience, emitting liquid ice into the body of the woman –

Sarah shifted her attention to the open books and a quick skim of text and pictures revealed the subject matter was all the same. Justin's bold hand had underscored in red ink the testimony from a seventeenth century witchcraft trial in red ink. Sarah leaned over it, her brow knitting.

He came and lay with me, and though he had the countenance of my husband, I knew it was not him. However, I could not resist him, so tempting was he to my weak woman's nature... As he...pierced me, his body and face changed, and became most hideous.

I screamed and struggled, and I angered it. I became filled with such coldness, a coldness like the deepest winter, and knew I should die there, frozen to death, lest I figure out some way to fight and get away. My neighbor came, and the creature vanished, but not in time to save three of my fingers and all of the toes of my right foot, which succumbed to the ice.

Sarah heard Justin's footsteps padding down the stairs and she turned.

He had just gotten out of the shower. Drops of water had collected at the tips of his hair and beaded onto his broad, pale shoulders. He held a towel loosely around his waist, slung low on his hips, the bare gesture of modesty for a man who thought he was alone in his home, and so had no reason to hide the brand on his lower abdomen, just above the line of his pubic area. The raised, damaged skin formed the same mark Lorraine Messenger had deliberately tattooed in the same place on her body.

"I know about the connection between you and Lorraine," Sarah said, lifting her eyes from that mark to his startled face. "So I know you're a lying bastard. What I want to know is if you're a murdering bastard as well."

The flash of surprise vanished into an unreadable expression that sent a searing coldness through her, comparable to what had been described in the text behind her. "Trust me, Herne," she snarled. "Now is not the time to play dark and mysterious with me. You're about two seconds from being charged with murder. As it is, I'm here to take you to Wassler for formal questioning."

"I didn't lie to you, Sarah," he said, his voice harsh. "I told you there were things I couldn't tell you, because you wouldn't believe me, and other things I wouldn't tell you, because they had nothing to do with the murder."

"And I told *you*, cops have a funny way of preferring to decide for themselves what relates to a murder." She swept a book up off the desk and flung it at his feet. It landed with the cover spread out like wings over the crushed pages. "Is this the truth I won't believe, Herne? Some delusion from the seventeenth century to cover your ass? No more bullshit. You took a piece of the victim's hair. You told me it was while I was with you. But how do I know that wasn't a lie, that you took it off her after you killed her? You hid what she was to you. Why would you hide this stuff from me? I'm good enough to fuck but not good enough to tell the truth to?"

"Is that what this is about? *Now* you want to act like we're in a real relationship where I owe you honesty, instead of continuing your childish pretense that we're just acting on our lust?"

She acted before she thought. She slapped him. She could have punched him, because she packed a good left, but she chose the ultimate blow of disdain and disappointment for a woman.

He stood still, they both did, for several silent moments that ached with things far more potent than had been said.

"You really think," he spoke at last, between clenched teeth. "You really think that I would come to the police chief's home after I murdered this woman, to give you any potential clues, like dirt on my feet, or unusual scratches on my skin? A police chief who saw me engaged in a similar ritual?"

"I don't know, Justin. Murderers aren't predictable. Maybe you thought by seducing me the same night, I'd be too embarrassed or distracted to implicate you."

"You must think I have the confidence of a god to have gone to your home with a diabolical plan to seduce a woman I'd never even met."

He did. That was the problem.

He saw it in her face and stepped forward, took her shoulders in hard hands before she could throw him off. "I know you don't believe for one second that I did this, but by thinking I did, you can build a wall against me and punish yourself for letting yourself be who you are. Why are you so damned scared of me, Sarah?"

"Because you want the control," she lashed out. "Because I can't keep my head on straight around you!"

"Sarah, you keep your head on straight during your job. You don't need to do it with me, here in this room. Ever. That's the point of a relationship. You both give up your control, you learn to trust someone else with your heart."

"We barely even know each other."

He caught her chin in his hand so she had to look up at him, meet his steady, intense gaze. "Yes, we do, Sarah. That's what frightens you. You were with a man for ten years and during that whole time you didn't feel an inkling of the intimacy with him that you feel just standing in my shop and exchanging a glance with me across twenty feet. That was his loss, and I won't mourn it, because I want you. I want to find out if our fate is forever, or just a short time of paradise, but you won't deny there's more here than sex, because I won't allow you to lie to me."

"But you lied to me. You said what you knew wasn't relevant." She wrested away. "You being the father of Lorraine Messenger's child, taking that child away from the mother, that seems awfully damned relevant."

He turned away, and that gauntness to his face became a haggard weariness. "She was not her mother," he said. "She bore her, but she never wanted her. Even when she came here three months ago, it was for me, not for our daughter. She was attracted to power, which she perceived that I had. I chose to deepen my practice in the Wiccan path when I lost my Lori. It had the answers my heart needed to heal, and I found it called to a place deep within me. When someone discovers the right spiritual path for themselves, they feel as if they've found a home for their soul. I found mine there."

He rubbed a hand over his face. "If you'll let me get over to the computer, I'll show you more. I don't suppose you'd allow me to put on some clothes?"

"Talk first, get decent later. Trust me, your manly body isn't going to overwhelm me."

He gave her an arch look and stalked past her. She tensed as he slid against her body in the small space. Despite her words, the closeness of the area made her stomach muscles tighten and tremble with emotions. He stopped there before her, and she made herself look up into his face, close enough for a kiss. The heat of his body, that almost supernatural warmth that both attracted and enveloped her, did both now, and made the pain almost unbearable.

"Stop whatever the hell it is you're doing to me," she snapped. "Show me the goddamned information."

"I'm not trying to do anything, Sarah," he said, and his dark eyes showed a pain she wanted to ignore. "The truth is the truth, whether it's the truth about Lorraine and me, or the truth about you and me."

He turned before she could shoot her denial at him, and sat in the chair in front of the computer. The towel parted, showing an expanse of thigh up almost to his hip. The sight of that part of his flesh disturbed her even more than his bare chest and back, still damp from his shower. It was somehow more intimate, that length of leg so close to his cock. Knowing that body had been hers to enjoy, had pleasured her. Knowing she wanted it still, and the man within it.

Step back, Sarah. Not physically. There was no room for that behind the desk. Her admonishment was for her jumbled emotions. She had to take a deep breath and establish some space in her overwrought mind to listen to him objectively. She could not leap to assumptions about his guilt simply because she was so afraid he was. No more than she could assume he was innocent because she desperately wanted him to be.

She very deliberately slid a hip onto the desk, crossed her arms. Herne nodded, as if he had been waiting for this physical cue that he had her attention.

"An incubus is a demon," he said, gesturing to the image on the computer screen. "Prior to Christianity's influence, a demon was simply a term for an otherworldly being. It could have been good or evil, a guide, teacher, or even an angel, as easily as it could have been a manifestation of darkness. It might even be good-bad neutral. An incubus's specialty is seducing women and impregnating them with the semen of human males, whether for good or bad purposes, it's hard to say. They obtain the semen by shifting..."

"I read that part."

"Eight years ago, I had the most vivid sexual experience of my life." A bitter smile touched his lips. "Until recently, I didn't think it could be matched. I dreamed of a woman, and in that dream, I made love to her. I expected to wake up a mess, like a teenager having a wet dream. It was obvious I had had an orgasm, but there was no semen, no fluids upon me except what I would expect if I had ejaculated into a woman's body." His tone became flat. "On my stomach was this brand. It hurt like hell. I could still smell the burning flesh. I saw a doctor about it, but he was helpless to explain the phenomenon."

The light from the desk lamp etched out his struggle to speak of the demons of his past. In this case, Sarah realized the description was literal, at least in Herne's mind. The jury was still out for her, but her hair was standing on her arms in an uncomfortable way.

"Nine months later, I got a call from a hospital in North Carolina. They had a pregnant woman there, a drug addict. In the pain of her labor and the delirium of her withdrawal, she screamed out my name as the father of the child, as well as the town in which I lived. The hospital found me.

"I'm curious, so I go and see the woman. Her face is the face of my dream, only in my dreams her face is unravaged by the drugs, as she might have been before she got hooked. The real woman does not have the overwhelming seductive power of the being of my dream. I'm shaken enough by the similarity, however, that I submit to a DNA test. The baby is ours."

Sarah sucked in a breath. Justin leaned back in the chair, splaying his knees, and stared at the screen and the image there, a macabre cartoon.

"I looked at this wreck of a woman, who had nothing but contempt for me and those around me. She did not know me, nor I her. Yet when I first came into her room, I saw she had some of the same sense of bewildering recognition of me as I did of her. I told the hospital I wanted to take custody of the child, for they had called social services in and refused to relinquish the child to her."

He reached out, rubbed at the side of the keyboard with his thumb, an absent gesture, a distraction for the emotions Sarah felt vibrating off of him. She saw his throat work as he swallowed. "When they let me hold her for the first time, and Lori looked at me, I knew we were bound. It was a miracle she came out healthy, that Lorraine didn't lose her or abort her before labor. Perhaps it was the circumstances of her birth that provided her some type, I don't know. Lorraine couldn't sign her over to me fast enough, was delighted I was willing to take her. She was so out of her head and confused by the whole situation. I was just as confused. She disappeared from the hospital the next day."

"You called the baby Lori."

He nodded. "I didn't know anything about Lorraine Messenger except she was a disaster, but I wanted to give the child the safest gift from her birth mother I could give her.

"I researched the brand, and that's where I found this." He scrolled down and she was looking at the same symbol in bold grey, red and black graphics as it had been tattooed on Lorraine's skin and burned into Justin's.

"If you go into the works of the monks of the sixteenth and seventeenth century, they did a detailed chronology and hierarchy of the angels and demons. This was in there. It also came up several times in testimony at witch trials. I uncovered another reference to it in a story written in the nineteenth century, a nickel pulp fiction by a cowboy in Colorado. Almost the exact story as mine. The dream, waking up with the brand. Three years later, he's in Colorado and meets an unmarried Indian maiden with the same mark, and her face is the one from his dream. She has a tattoo like his brand, that she felt compelled to have one of the tribe stencil on her in the same spot. She has a boy who looks so much like the cowboy, there's no doubt it has to be his son."

Justin scrolled down as he spoke, so Sarah's attention covered the same detail information he was referencing. He pointed to a smaller photo of the horned and fanged caricature at the top. The rendering of the monks, their belief of his true form. To most of his victims he appears with the face of a person they know, or as an attractive, seductive stranger that they might later discover or meet.

"The Indian woman and cowboy married and lived happily ever after in the fictional account. The woman in the witch trial was exonerated for succumbing to the influence of the Devil, but her husband cast her and her child out of his home and she was expelled from the community. There are reports she joined her sister in Virginia and became a shopkeeper, her son a respected attorney. And you know my story, and Lorraine's."

"But why would it do this? What purpose—"

"I expect it's simply a random, unhappy spirit." Justin lifted a shoulder. "There's a theory that, just the same way we long to connect to or possess the powers of supernatural beings, so, too, do those beings sometimes wish to connect with or possess characteristics of our mortality. This may be a way to do it."

Sarah chewed on the inside of her cheek, studied the screen. "Say I believe any of this, and that's a big 'if'. Did you find any evidence of it actually killing someone in the way Lorraine was killed?"

"Six times in the past century." He confirmed her fears, flipping to another screen where she saw various news articles that had been downloaded from library archive files. He maintained his silence as she quickly read through the data he had compiled. Different parts of the world, always at least ten or fifteen years apart, sometimes much longer.

"He's been around for awhile," Justin said. "He doesn't always kill, and there's no indication of why he does, just that he has a short fuse and a lot of power. He's killed four women, two men. The only clue is in that seventeenth century account. As far as I can tell, she's the only one who ever survived him when he got angry. And she's the only one who ever recorded seeing him as an image similar to the rendering of the monks."

"You've been researching this for some time," she said, realizing the impact of that even as her gaze swept the stacks of files on his desk, the books on paranormal phenomena on his shelves.

"Since it happened to me, over eight years ago. It shocked the hell out of me, the day you took me to the murder site. Seeing Lorraine dead was terrible, but not unexpected. It was hard to see the body, though. To remember..." He moved the mouse to keep the monitor from switching to the screensaver.

"What shocked you, then?" Sarah prompted him.

"That she was trying to call it. It never occurred to me that she ever had the cognizance to recognize the incubus was more than a bad trip, but apparently she did. She was Wiccan. In her lucid moments, few and far between though they may have been, she put it together." Justin's mouth thinned, the lips pressed hard together. "She was near bottom when she came to see me several months ago. Maybe she thought if she could get pregnant by it again, I would give her money." He swiveled in the chair, looked up at Sarah, "Or maybe she just wanted to feel that good again for a few minutes. But as I said, this demon's got a short fuse. I suspect he doesn't care for being called or ordered about."

"Or," she responded, "maybe he saw it as a mercy killing, she was so far gone."

Justin leaned forward, rubbed a hand over his face. "I'll go with you to Eric's office, Sarah, but I'm not going to tell him all this. If you want to do it, fine, but you can see now that there's nothing the police can do to stop this thing, even if you all believed me."

"What will kill it?"

"You can't kill a demon. It's pure energy. You can neutralize it, bind it, lock it into a contained space in the universe. The coven can do that, but to do it we'd have to find him and close in around him before he knew we were coming, and this guy has no pattern as to whom he chooses initially for his victim. He shows up whenever, wherever."

He rose out of the chair so his back was to her, and stepped back out of the desk space.

"I'll go get dressed."

Sarah stared after him for several long moments. Her brain had gone as numb as her heart and she wasn't sure how long she stood there, paralyzed, before the cell phone at her belt rang.

She pulled it off. "Wylde here,"

"This is Dexter, Sarah." Her lieutenant's voice was a rush of relieved words. "They finally got the rest of the dang reports from the medical examiner. Forensics says the vic's death was self-inflicted. They didn't find any evidence of another person at the scene. No footprints, hair or skin samples on her clothes or belongings. Not even any semen in her body or evidence of a condom. There were three drugs in her system. She was a freaking pharmacy. The toxicologist played with the combination and came up with a reaction like liquid nitrogen. It's something he's never seen before, but when it all comes together, it turns into negative 100 degrees immediately. He says we may have a new street drug, or she may have hit on something by accident with her little cocktail. He said based on that and a totally clean site, Marion's just got themselves a really freaky OD situation."

"Is that his official medical opinion?"

Dexter hesitated. "Sorry about that, Chief. His official report is going to rule it an OD death. Another thing, even better news. Time of death was pinned at 11:00 pm. We have nine people who verified independently that Justin Herne was leading a Wiccan ritual from eight o'clock to midnight. Forensics says that alibis him even if he shot it into her veins and left her there for it to take effect."

Ten people, she thought.

"Chief?"

"Good work, Dexter. I'm at Herne's home now. I'll inform him and then I'm off for the rest of the day. I think I've got a touch of the flu."

"Yes ma'am, that's been going around. We're all glad about the way it turned out, though, but sorry for that lady. She sure was messed up."

"Yes, she was. Bye, Dexter."

Sarah stood there, listening to the sounds of Herne moving upstairs, drawers opening and closing. She looked at the computer screen again, the fanged creature sneering at her.

When Justin came down a few minutes later, his sitting room was empty, and Sarah's car was gone. A scrap of paper was propped up on the computer screen, held there with a piece of tape. The shadow of the demon was silhouetted behind it.

Justin pulled off the note and swore viciously.

You've been cleared. We're through.

"That's what you think, sweetheart," he growled, crushing the note in his hand.

Chapter 14

ಜ

He let her be for the night. He could be that patient, knowing the weight of what he had laid on her earlier in the day. He did leave a message on her machine, he couldn't help that.

"Sarah, this is Justin. We're going to have to talk about us. There *is* an 'us', whether you want there to be or not, and I want to see you. Call me tomorrow, or I swear I'll show up on your doorstep and you'll have to deal with me. I should have handled things differently, I know, but don't use it as an excuse to run from me. Don't run from us."

He lay in bed for awhile staring at the ceiling, and then gave up and snapped on the small reading light. He withdrew the news clippings he had printed from the Chicago Times and went through them again, imagining Sarah all alone in a warehouse full of blood and violence, her struggle toward that one last man, her refusal to give up.

From Sarah's limited comments on her personal life, Justin knew her husband had left her shortly thereafter. He had left her when she needed him desperately, and it sounded like during their marriage he had let her push him away when she thought the job had become too much to share. Justin wasn't going to let her do it to him. She needed someone in her life strong enough to push back.

He turned off the light, lay back in the bed and went back to studying the ceiling until the grandfather clock downstairs struck midnight, and his body raged for her. He wondered if this was how drugs had been for Lorraine, this all-consuming need to have that pleasure in her blood. He wanted Sarah in his house, in his arms. He wanted his cock buried in her and her body arching beneath his, that sinuous movement that women made, an erotic dance to offer themselves up to a man's need, to sate their own in the bonding.

Fuck it. He was going to get up and go to her house, and he was going to use every method, fair or unfair, to get her to accept him. He knew it was wrong, but he didn't give a damn. He hadn't believed he would ever know what love felt like again, and certainly hadn't expected it to take the form of an instantaneous attachment to a skinny police chief with a smart mouth, shy smile and irises as big as robin eggs.

He flipped over and jumped back with a startled oath. Sarah was in the process of getting into his bed, her knee up to slide in next to him. Justin froze, his face just inches from hers. She stared back, her eyes round and sad, and her lips parted to speak. He caught her to him, his hand to the back of her head, and brought her to his lips. He nearly moaned at the joy of that contact, her bare breasts crushed against his chest, for she was naked as he was, her body cool where his was hot, a melding of elements.

"I'm sorry," he muttered against her, and she made a noise of acceptance. He was already achingly hard for her, and she straddled him with her thighs, pulling the sheet back and sliding down on him, taking him inside her, fusing them together even with their lips still joined. He wanted to touch her, caress her, watch her grow more and more wild with passion, but she seemed as desperate to simply mate as he did. She left him no choice, for the muscles in her cunt clamped down on him. As she rose and fell on his body, riding that wave of their desire, she was as relentless as a rider mounted on a thoroughbred, coaxing him with the stroke of her silken walls to lengthen his stride, make for the finish line.

"Sarah, let me—"

She shook her head, placing her fingers over his lips. He groaned again as her hands lifted, cupped her breasts, their quivering movement contained in the curve of her palms, her nipples stiff and eager. He reared up to possess them with his lips and tongue.

He dug his fingers into her waist, moving his grip up to either side of her spine, then back down, clutching her hips. Even as he realized something was wrong, his body refused to acknowledge the warning. His frustration and pent up desire for Sarah exploded, the orgasm ripping through him, leaving him torn between horror and pain.

He had only known Chief Sarah Wylde for two days, but Justin Herne was a man who noticed details, not just as a shopkeeper, but as a man who revered that which was precious. Under his right palm, he knew there was supposed to be the smooth, satin circle of a bullet scar. There was none.

He snarled his frustration as his cock was milked dry by the being upon him. As his hands clutched in an involuntary clamp on its hips, the Sarah image wavered and he saw the being's true eyes, the eyes he had seen in Lorraine's face so many years ago, when what he had thought had been a dream had led to the best miracle and worst nightmare of his life.

"Don't," Justin gasped, "Don't—"

The Sarah creature shook its head, put its hands over Justin's at its hips, then the touch was gone.

Justin blinked. He was alone, the incubus gone, only the tangled sheets and trembling post-orgasmic state of his body telling him what had just transpired was real. Even that would not have convinced him, if he had not been father to an angel because of a similar visit over eight years ago.

He rolled over, grabbed the phone, knocked it off its pedestal. "Son of a—" He scrambled for it, snatched it up. The phone rang and rang, and he swore again when he got Sarah's machine. "Sarah, this is Justin. Pick up. Please, it's urgent. It's about the murder."

He waited, snarled when she did not pick up the phone. He broke the connection, made the call to the uniform working dispatch in Lilesville on graveyard shift.

"She called about an hour ago," the rookie said. "Said she was still feeling under the weather and wouldn't likely be in this morning."

"Where'd she call from?"

"She said she was at home."

All the alarm bells went off. In Justin's gut, his head, in every nerve and musclem, including the ones that tightened his grip on the phone until his knuckles whitened. "Thanks."

He held the buzzing receiver against his forehead for a long moment. He might be overreacting, but his intuition told him he wasn't. It told him he needed help and Sarah needed protection, fast. Lori had been born almost nine months to the day from when the incubus first visited him. When it took semen, it went immediately to the person whose form it had assumed. That was the only clue to a pattern they had, and that person would be Sarah.

His first reaction was to protect her, to call the rookie back and say whatever he needed to say to get the entire force screaming over to her house with sirens and lights blazing. The police would be able to scare off the incubus, but they would not be able to anticipate the next victim.

Inexplicably, his gaze fell on the article from the *Chicago Times* that he had left out. He remembered Sarah's face as she talked to the kids about drugs, not in a condescending way, but in the way someone talked who really cared, who believed that she was responsible for every face out in that audience.

"*...we'd have to find him and close in around him before he knew we were there.*"

Sarah was a police officer, sworn to protect and serve. She would want to protect her people, and the people in this town were his as well. He and the coven were the only ones capable of stopping the thing, but the cost might be Sarah's life.

"No, damn it." He erupted from the bed, grabbing for the nearest pair of pants. "It's not taking her. It's not."

He hit the preset button to dial Linda as he took the stairs to the lower level three at a time. "Oh, God, Sarah," he murmured as he listened to the ring. "Hang on, baby. I'm coming."

* * * * *

He couldn't possibly have the nerve to break into her house again.

Who was she kidding? This was Justin Herne, the man of steel when it came to nerve. Defying a homicide investigation, telling the cop in charge he would pick and choose what information he cared to divulge, fucking the sheriff in the neighboring county half-blind, making her fall for him.

She shrugged irritably into her robe. She should take her gun, but he might interpret that as a sentimental gesture.

How fondly would he think of it if she actually shot him this time? In a place where it might do some good.

She really needed to start locking that door. Bolting it. Booby trapping it with hot oil and barbed spikes.

Sarah moved up the hallway and saw firelight. Despite the warming weather, she had built a fire earlier in the evening. She had been feeling a cold in her bones that came as much from the drain of her turbulent emotions as her lack of body fat. It had been embers when she went to bed, but apparently he had stoked it up, thinking that the romantic gesture would warm her. He was in for a surprise. It was going to take the fires of hell to melt the icy frost she felt for him right now.

She stepped into her sitting room and he turned from where he stood before the fire.

It was a good thing she hadn't brought the gun, because it would have dropped from nerveless fingers.

He was naked, long muscles outlined and praised by the fire, from the taut right buttock on which he rested most of his weight to the smooth landscape across his broad back. A wave of desire struck her, so strong it made her knees weak. Attraction vibrated beneath his skin, called to her body as nothing ever had, so her pussy immediately pulsed at high alert, as if seconds away from climax.

It was Justin. It wasn't Justin. Two parts of her brain processed what her eyes saw and spat out entirely different data. Unfortunately, the part that told her it was Justin was in charge of her body, moving it forward toward the being from which her heart screamed she should retreat.

The dark eyes beckoned her with no more than a flicker of movement, a slight curve of that sensual mouth that she could already imagine moving over her skin, branding, sucking, kissing, biting, marking her, leaving no crevice unexplored. Her pussy tightened, her breasts ached, and when he reached out, his long fingers closing over her wrist, she shuddered, a quivering sigh escaping her.

"Sarah," he whispered. "I want you."

He's a stranger. He's the incubus.

"I want you. Only you. I can make everything not matter. Don't fight me. I only want to bring you pleasure like you've never known."

His hands moved over her shoulders, curled in the neck of her robe, peeled it back over her shoulders. Sarah stood in his armspan, feeling his cool hands on her skin, the firelight behind him warming her calves. His touch was ten times more potent than his gaze, and the moment his fingers slid over her breasts she came, hard, her fingers gripping his arms in shock as she rocked forward on her toes, her forehead pressed against his chest. He did no more than tweak her nipples gently, prolonging the climax. Her arousal ran down her legs and he caught some of it in his other hand that dipped between her legs and found her.

She writhed, her body still spasming from the aftershock of one climax even as he started stroking her impossibly toward a second.

"You're mine, Sarah." Justin's face and voice filled her senses. She was headed to the floor, her body held in his arms. She didn't fight. She couldn't. "You're too precious a gift for this world. I think you belong in mine."

Her will shrieked at her body to move, to resist. She had read stories of people put under for surgery who didn't go under but were paralyzed, unable to tell the doctor they were awake and feeling everything. Or pets, tranquilized for airline flight, too lethargic to move but terrified to the bone.

An icy ball of terror surrounded her will, watching her body offer itself to a being she knew was not Justin, hearing his words and knowing what they meant. She was unable to do more than observe herself willingly and eagerly open herself to him as he lowered himself between her thighs, his cock erect and potent. It brushed her and she cried out, a sound of pleasure that ricocheted off the scream of denial inside her head.

Being in control was important to a cop, important to Sarah. Perversely, she had gone into situations where she knew control of the outcome wasn't possible. But she was always able to be in control of herself, of Sarah. The day she had dragged herself to her feet and made it across fifty feet of blood-soaked concrete floor, she had known her life was likely about to be taken from her. However, she still had the choice. She could cross that floor to do the job or run.

Justin had known her fear of that loss of self from the beginning. So even when he cuffed her to her bed, there had been that still moment, that tender kiss, that acknowledgement of her, who she was, her soul. His own had reached out to touch it, so that what they were doing had been something they were doing to each other, even though she had been scared to death and more aroused than she'd ever been in her life.

Until now. But this was different. There was no pause, no touching of souls, not even a chance to catch her breath. He was yanking her body's reaction from her like a doctor using a hammer on her knee joints, driving her up and over pinnacles at breakneck speed before she was ready for them, a spiraling whirlwind where the orgasms were just leading to even more gripping climaxes, an ocean of heat suddenly invaded by ice as he drove into her. The contrast brought forth another orgasm that wrenched open something inside her that shouldn't be opened. Her scream was torn between pleasure and pain, leaving her nowhere to hide or run.

The cold spread through her and she shuddered in the grip.

His cock drove into her with such force their bodies moved backwards on the hearth rug. Her hair, trapped under her shoulders, tugged her head back so he could sink his teeth into her throat. Her traitorous legs rose, clasped around his hips, her breath panting, lips moist from the cold breath coming from between his. His hands moved down her sides, over her ribs, under her to cup her breasts, then between their bodies to stroke her clit at their joining.

"Come for me again, Sarah. Hard. Bring my come into you, milk me for your pleasure."

She now understood how much power she had held. Justin had desired her, wanted her, overwhelmed her with her body's responses to him. But it had been *her* response always, not something he manipulated from her as she had accused him of doing. She might have held onto that cowardly belief if she didn't have this moment to compare it to. She had wanted what he had been offering, fiercely.

Pleasure. Warmth. Affection. Friendship. All the potentials for love had been in his touch, his eyes and his voice from the very beginning, and time and rationality had had nothing to do with it. Her heart had known from the first moment, and had joined with her body and soul in responding to the same remarkable response from his.

This being had locked her heart and soul away from her body, and those elements were prisoners inside her head as all the sensual centers of her physical self rose up in response to his seductive powers. They dragged the rest of her screaming toward the icy abyss the cold darkness of his eyes promised.

Oh, God. Justin, help me.

Chapter 15

﹩

The bastard had somehow taken or hidden his car keys.

He didn't want to delay Linda in getting to Sarah with the coven, so Justin took the forest paths. He had not bothered with a shirt, so the perspiration gleamed on his shoulders. His bare feet pounded the earth, and blood roared in his ears. He felt the texture of Sarah's skin under his damp palms, the scent of her hair brush his nose and mouth as he drew in gulps of air. Her blue eyes, wary, distrustful. Glazed with desire. Her smile. Her quiet words to him in the deepest part of the night, murmured against his ear as her arms came around his shoulders.

She was his. His to love, his to protect. Danger was a scent around her that grew with every stride he made toward her, fueling his body's speed until there was no hesitation in his movements, even when his instincts guided him off the path to take a more direct route to her house. His spirit rose within him, pulling on the energies of the night, the energies that were a part of him. His legs lengthened, grew even stronger. He felt the weight of the antlers on his skull, weapons of defense as much as the flashing dark hooves and the powerful muscles that gathered and sailed him over fallen trees in his path. He was an eternal force of protection, the will of man and God coming together for one purpose. To save life, and love. To protect.

He heard the chanting as he got closer. He broke from the clearing behind Sarah's home and saw them, five women in contemporary dress, everything from hastily pulled on jeans to nightshirts and slippers. Appearance had been irrelevant. They had come immediately, knowing what they faced. They drew toward the house from the five cardinal points, shrinking the circle, binding what was inside the four walls of that cottage. Justin sensed the creature, knew it was there, and rage filled his senses.

He brayed out a challenge that reverberated through the clearing. Linda's eyes widened as the stag leaped over the boundary of the circle and charged past, the points of his antlers glowing like swords in the moonlight, his hooves cutting across the earth with lethal purpose.

"Great Lady," one of the coven murmured.

"Blessed Lord," Linda whispered. The stag gathered itself and leaped. He went through the front bay window, glass exploding like shards of rain and shimmering on the beast's withers. The powerful melding of Justin and Herne, the forest god, stormed forward to protect what was theirs.

"Take the circle inside," Linda cried out, running forward.

* * * * *

Sarah lay before the fire, her beautiful body bare and licked by the firelight, the incubus buried between her legs. Justin saw all this as he crashed through the window. His momentum did not slow. He moved forward in a run as the incubus pulled out of her body and leaped up. They met over Sarah's inert form.

The creature seized his antlers to slow his charge. Justin was aware his form had shifted again, so now he had the appearance he had in the circle, only instead of a costume, he was still a genuine melding of man and stag, with human legs and arms but the strength and antlered deer head of Herne. The tawny hair of the stag ran in a stripe down the center of his broad back.

Justin's rage propelled them both back to the wall and he pinned the incubus there for a moment. The incubus dissolved and reformed outside of the cage of the antlers.

Between Sarah's legs, he had possessed Justin's appearance, but now as he rematerialized he took his own face. It was not what the monks recorded. He had the form of a tall and handsome man, the man he had once been on the mortal plane, though in the being's eyes Justin saw the hatred that had turned to evil intent. Perhaps the monks and those who had died or almost died at his hands, being so close to God, had seen his inside as his outside.

"You lost what I gave you last time," the incubus spat, and Justin heard the words in his mind, as well as aloud. "You become greedy."

"I won't lose her to you," Justin responded grimly. "She should be allowed to choose. You shouldn't be allowed to take that from her. And you're trapped here. You can't leave."

Linda and the summoned members of the coven slid into the room, one through the open shattered window, two from the hallway entrance, two from the kitchen entrance, keeping the circle locked in place.

The creature's gaze darted around the room, and Justin felt him throw out his senses, test the strength of the binding. A moment of panic warred with fury on the incubus's face. "Will you keep me locked in your circle forever? You can fight me and I will never tire, but even with the force of Herne called into you, your human body will fail you. She will still be mine, and though I'm bound in this circle, they will not be able to stop me from taking her life."

Justin looked toward the fire where Sarah lay on the rug. Her eyes were vacant, her body sinuously moving, still responding to the impact of the incubus on her senses, but he could also see the rigidity of her shoulders, the tightness of her face, and knew she was in there, fighting. Losing.

The rage died from his eyes, replaced by hard purpose. "You're right." He nodded, stepping back. "This isn't about you and me, anyway. This is about me and Sarah."

He turned his shoulder to the incubus and bent over Sarah, letting the strength of Herne go, so the flesh that came against Sarah's flesh was all human, all Justin. Her eyes focused, blinked hazily, and he was there, holding her, his hands on either side of her face so she could look into his eyes.

"Sarah," he said urgently.

She vaguely felt Linda's presence, her and the other women. Justin's words penetrated her mind, forcing her to grapple with the situation.

"Trust me, Sarah," he demanded. "Whatever else we are, you know when I hold you what it is between us. Trust me. Follow me."

She had little other choice in this moment, but she knew, looking up into his serious eyes, that she *could* trust him. He had not been completely truthful with her, but it was clear that now was the time to accept and forgive, even if she could not understand.

"Okay," she whispered, and forcing that word over her vocal cords was the hardest thing she had ever done, as if the acknowledgement had to be dragged from under a pile of rocks at the bottom of the deepest part of the ocean. A wisp of pleasure trickled through her mind at the flare of approval in his eyes. She was so tired and yet so aroused at once, willing and wanting him to do anything with her, and she would let him, drifting in a haze of pleasure and dreams.

His eyes darkened and the handsome blonde man beside him moved. No, melded…no, it was like two blurry images coming together, only they hadn't been blurry, but now they were one. It was Justin's hands touching her, but she felt them both, two presences kissing her lips, but Justin was in the forefront. The other was just a pleasurable, non-alarming shadow that added caresses in places that one person could not caress all at once. She felt hands on her breasts, and a mouth sucking them even as Justin kissed her lips, and his hands slid down to her hips, parted her legs. She gasped, bowing up as if touched by fire, for now his hand was there, his fingers, but so was another's, heat balanced with cold.

"Take us both in, Sarah, flesh, warmth and ice, rousing her nerves with the contrast life and death. You're the one that can bring the balance."

She felt them, one overlaid on the top of the other, but just enough off rhythm that the slide into her body had a double stroke to it, the ridge of two heads rubbing her flesh, heat and cold, rousing her nerves with the contrast. Justin's arms were around her. Justin, warm, solid, real. Though the other was there, too, powerful, mesmerizing, arousing, he had nothing to offer her heart. The more she opened to Justin, the more she felt what he could give to her, would give to her, if she'd only let go of her fears.

Her back curved up as she felt the incubus's mouth on her, just over where Justin thrust into her. That mouth sucked her clit even as Justin's cock found the right place deep inside her. Fingers crept under her, caressing her, making her open wider. The two temperatures shivered up her nerve endings and set off a spasm of ripples in her lower belly.

The incubus had his hands on her breasts, while Justin's chest rubbed them with his slow, deliberate movements. The incubus quickened, a seesaw inside her juxtaposed to Justin's slow, pumping strokes.

Her body was overloading on sensations, hovering on the edge of explosive orgasm, but there was so much, she couldn't. There was something wrong with it, like a vibrator on so high it was deadening the same nerves it was intending to stimulate. She felt like she was in a choke hold and she could not draw breath to make the leap.

She was open to both beings, man and spirit, but more than her body was being called by one of the men. It was toward that one her soul turned in desperation. She felt it, as she knew she had felt it that first over-the-top night with him. The power of Earth, of the Divine. Of a Fate that could not be denied. Him. Her.

"Sarah," Justin whispered, his eyes glittering like the blade of a weapon. "Let go for me, Sarah. Feel me within you. Just the heat. My body against yours, my cock within you, my hands on your body. That's all there is, just the two of us."

The chanting of the women increased, and the power emanated off Justin as he used it, gave her breathing room, cleared a space in her mind she needed. His face muscles quivered with the effort. She reached up, pushed through the thick presence of the incubus between them and cupped his jaw in her hand. "Kiss me, Justin. Please...before I die."

"You're not going to die," he said fiercely, and he plunged through the incubus's spirit as if he were smoke and covered her mouth with his own.

Heat, wet, life. Demanding she live, he caught the fading strands of her strength with his, wrapped them around his consciousness, binding her to him, and drove them both off the edge of that pinnacle.

Sarah screamed with the force of it, and it was just his force, for the flood of liquid heat inside her brooked no intrusion. He used the power and resistance in her soul with his own magic to call whatever power would aid them, bringing the Lord and Lady down into their coupling and shoving the incubus back on his heels, outside their joining which had no place for him, into the cold prison of the circle.

The magic grew as the climax continued, and Justin's gaze flicked briefly up to Linda, just behind Sarah's head. The witch nodded and the tone of her chant changed, a chorus of destruction and creation both, two parts of the whole.

The incubus snarled and tried to escape, charging at the circle's boundary, but the women had joined hands and the binding held firm. For a moment he became more solid, the image of the corporeal form he had been again. A handsome man carrying his hatred stamped on his face and on his existence. His body began to fade, and Sarah's glazed eyes registered the gradual impression of the firelight shining through his form.

Justin chanted softly, firmly against Sarah's ear as he continued to stroke within her, hard and strong. In between the words she heard his murmured caress to her.

"Mine."

Sarah clung to him, simply held on as the aftershocks of her climax rippled through her with each stroke. She desperately clung to the light that was him, her promise of life, of survival.

The incubus wailed. The coven grimly continued its work. His body's transparent state began to blur, a fading into amorphous colors. Tendrils of his form grasped at Justin's shoulders, but they lost their purchase as the cloud of energy floated upward, still within the circle's boundary, but with no control of its direction any longer.

"There is hope for you, demon," Linda's voice resonated through the room, and the power of the Goddess was in her face.

"You have been rendered powerless on this plane. You are no more than a seductive whisper in a woman's ear, able to turn her heart only for a passing thought. You no longer have the power to command mortal souls to your will, or transfer the seed of men to her womb. If you ever wish to be more than a shadow again, ever wish to achieve the grace of a new life blessed by My Love, you shall have to find that foundation you lack, and suffer and sacrifice for it, until you rectify your past harm.

"I pitied your pain, but transgressions demand recompense. Go, my child."

In an eerie movement, very un-Linda like, the priestess raised her hand, her two fingers crooked, and waved him away. His form dissolved as if swallowed by the air.

Sarah was suddenly conscious of the hum of her air conditioner, the refrigerator in the kitchen, the icemaker tumbling more cubes into the catch tray. Innocuous, comforting sounds. She was also aware of a pounding in her head that was growing stronger, overwhelming everything else, including the weakening beat of her heart.

"Justin," she whispered. "Hold me. I'm so cold."

They had been too late to save her, but they had defeated the incubus. He wouldn't hurt anyone again. Sarah accepted that, too tired to do anything else. The world became Justin's alarmed face, then just his eyes. Her life force slipped out of her, a breath against the press of his lips onto hers. She wished she had the strength to touch his face once more. Darkness closed in, and all wishes faded into dreams.

Chapter 16

ဆာ

Beeping. She knew what beeping meant. It meant you were alive, barely. When she woke up in the hospital after the drug shooting, she had learned how badly she was hurt by the erratic rate of that beeping heart monitor. She had learned first off that the fact she was aware of the beeping was good, very good, no matter how offbeat or slow it was.

This was slow, but the rhythm tended to increase once consciousness came, because that was when the pain hit. She wasn't disappointed.

The gunshot wounds had been a centralized focus of the agony that radiated throughout her system. This was a throbbing ache with no source point, as if her entire body had been tumbled down a hill in a drum.

"Hurts." She whispered it, and tears rolled out of her eyes at just that movement.

"I know, baby. I'm here."

His hand on hers, his voice rough with emotion. No man had ever thought to call her baby, ever thought she might need that. Hell, she hadn't thought she needed it. But he had. He was there. He hadn't taken off, he had fought the bad guy with her. He had covered her back, her whole body if she wanted to get literal about it. He had been there, protected her, stopped evil.

"Don't go," she said, a breath of sound, but he was bent forward, close enough to hear.

"I won't."

* * * * *

Two weeks later, the hospital had pumped enough fluids and painkillers into Chief Sarah Wylde to give her body the chance to recover from the mysterious incident that had lowered her body temperature below freezing. Astonishingly, there had been no frostbite or amputation. The cold had simply stopped the function of her vital organs for a dangerous amount of time.

According to the police report, Justin Herne had found her in her home and had used CPR to keep her heart beating. Eric Wassler suspected he had used everything up to and including selling his soul to Satan to keep her alive.

Marion's police chief stood outside her door now. Pale as a ghost she was, but she was propped on some pillows and smiling at something the nurse had said. Justin had given them moment alone, choosing to stand in the hallway, but he hadn't gone far away. Wassler could still see him out of the corner of his eye, hovering in the waiting area.

Her men had sent all sorts of balloons and flowers that she'd finally been able to have in her room when they moved her out of the Gainesville critical care area.

She saw him and smiled wider, holding out her hand in a gesture of affection somewhat uncoplike, but permissible due to the circumstances, and since she was female. He was glad for it, for it gave him the chance to give her cheek a kiss and her frail body a hard hug.

"Damn, I didn't realize quite how much I liked you," he said roughly, holding her at arms' length. "Aren't they feeding you in here?"

She chuckled and waved at the assortment of chocolates. "I get to go back to solid foods Monday. My system is too weak to do digestion. I've been tempted to bolt down a box and just suffer the consequences, but the nurses have terrified me with graphic descriptions of throwing up my internal organs if I do one thing they don't tell me I can do. You should have come sooner."

"I did." He pressed her hand. He had visited her often as she hovered between life and death, one of many who had.

"I've been here before, Eric," she said, sobering. "I'm still not ready to go."

"Glad to hear it, but let's not test it again, okay? I think you've made your lifetime quota of near misses." He cleared his throat. "Sarah, I need to... I'm going to ask you once. I asked Justin, and he said it was for you to say. Your symptoms. The lowered temperature..."

She nodded. Her blue eyes had a serenity in them, he realized, something she hadn't had before. Her first brush with death and her divorce had brought her demons. Her second brush appeared to have dispelled them.

"It was the same thing, Eric. Justin was right. It wasn't something of this world, though I suspect it was created by it. It's gone now, thanks to Justin and the coven, and we don't...it's no longer a police matter. There won't be any more victims in our county, or anywhere else. Not from this perp."

He studied her for a long moment. He knew her to be level-headed, a great cop, and there wasn't a trace of delirium in her eyes, just practicality. He also knew if she thought there was still a threat, they'd be having to tie her to the bed to keep her from going after it.

"Okay," he said, and left it at that. The report on Lorraine Messenger was a closed file, and since Sarah was not filing a criminal report on her illness, so was this. He put a hand over hers again, squeezed. "You get back to work soon, hear? Dexter's getting delusions of grandeur, being in charge."

She grinned, and he tried to focus on the sparkle in her eyes versus the gauntness of her cheeks. "You bet. Is Justin still out there?"

"I don't think he's been further than a hundred feet from you since they brought you here," Eric said dryly. He grinned at the sudden pink tint of her cheeks. "You let me know if you want a restraining order filed, hear?"

* * * * *

It was several more days before Justin chose to expand that distance. Her parents were due in today, for against his wishes she had not permitted him to call them until now, when it was obvious she was going to pull through.

Justin pulled up a chair beside her. Sarah expected him to take her hand as he had so often, but he didn't. "I need to say something to you," he said.

For the first time in the short time they'd known each other, Justin Herne looked unsure of himself.

"A lot of things happened in those very few moments," he said at last. "They say the Lord and Lady can instill full enlightenment upon a mind in the space of a breath, but that the human mind is a sieve. I couldn't hold onto all of it, but I did get some of it. You're an incredible person, Sarah."

He should have reached for her hand then, but he didn't. She wondered why, for he was not acting emotionally distant. Quite the contrary. His eyes were full of need for her.

"An amazing, intelligent woman with a generous heart. I knew some of that, but on that plane I felt every aspect of who you are, who you've been, who you'll be. I realized how much I've taken from you when I should have been asking. You deserved to be courted. I wanted you, instantly and more desperately than I've ever wanted anything, except to get my daughter back. So I rolled over you, no different than that incubus, overwhelming you."

"Justin—"

He shook his head. "It's important I tell you this, Sarah. Hear me out. I did lie to you. Sin of omission is bullshit. The excuse that you wouldn't believe what I knew, also bullshit. I didn't tell you because I couldn't talk about it, wouldn't talk about it. Or Lorraine." He rubbed a hand over his face.

Sarah realized for the first time how exhausted he was. Why hadn't she noticed how pale he had become these last several weeks, how that gaunt hardness of his face had gotten more pronounced? She reached out, covered his hand, offered him comfort for a change.

"Justin, you don't need to say all this. You need to go home. Rest, eat a decent meal instead of some of this liquefied crap off my tray, and worry about yourself for a little while. You've seen me through the worst of it. I'm going to be okay."

He turned his hand, tightened his grip on hers until she winced and he let go, easing off immediately. "It was pride, Sarah. He took my choices away. He gave me my angel, but deep underneath all of that, he tricked me, forced my body, and that deeply offended me. Pissed me off. Disturbed the hell out of me. Whatever you want to call it."

A woman would have called it rape, a violation. It was even harder for a man to say it, particularly a man like Justin Herne. She had forgiven him for not revealing what had happened, but her forgiveness had come because he had been there in the desperate moments when it counted. Now Sarah let go any lingering distrust, because she truly understood his silence. She had seen his actions in relation to herself, never as a man who had been victimized. Seeing it in that light, his silence made perfect sense. She was hearing truth, at last.

"If I had told you sooner, maybe this wouldn't have happened."

"Was there any way to stop him, other than how you did it?" she asked.

"What?"

"You heard me. Was there any other way? You couldn't predict where he would go except that one instance, because you knew his pattern of going to the woman whose form he took."

"If I had had time to research—"

"Then he could have harmed someone else."

"Linda—"

"Would be in this bed instead of me. You think that I would accept that? I wear a badge, Justin. It's my job to protect."

"I know. I knew it that night. That's why…damn it." He started up out of the chair, walked over to the window and stood there, his shoulders rigid. "I could have told the dispatch rookie that someone was breaking into your home, anything, and the cavalry would have come and scared him away. But I didn't, because I knew you'd want to get him. Then I felt you die in my arms, and I knew I'd never forgive myself if I lost you."

"But you didn't lose me. You hung onto my soul, Justin, you wouldn't let it fly away. I am alive because of you. Please come back over here. Please." Her eyes were wet, and he came. She took his hand as he sat on the edge of her bed, and she held onto it with the same fervency with which he had poured his life into hers that night, keeping her breathing. "It's my job to protect. Just like it is yours." She laid her free hand over his heart and felt it beat beneath her touch. "You wear your badge here, but I can see it. I would have made the same choice, if it had been me."

"I didn't give you a choice when we met, Sarah. I took advantage of your every weakness to claim you as mine, didn't give you a chance to think it through. I still want you." His voice dropped and he flicked a glance at her, filled with that hunger. "But I'm going to step back and give you the time to think it through, time to choose."

"What?" Her brow furrowed. "You're leaving me?"

"No." His hand contracted on hers, that brief, hard grip. "I'm not going anywhere, Sarah. You want me as your lover, I'm all yours. You want a friend, you've got one. You need me just to be a shopkeeper in your jurisdiction," a muscle ticked under his eye, "-so be it. I took away your rights, Sarah, so I've got no claim on you until you want to make one on me. I want you, I'm here, and I'm not going anywhere, but I'm going to give you the time and space to make up your own mind."

He bent, pressed a kiss to her hand, then he brushed his mouth against her cheek, catching the corner of her ready, confused lips.

"Now, your parents are here. That's the other thing I came to tell you. I asked them to give me a couple minutes because I knew you'd want to make yourself presentable, but you're beautiful. You eat, grow strong again." He stood, looked down at her. "Lilesville needs you, and so do I."

* * * * *

Well, he certainly had a damn fine way of showing it. A week passed, then another. He did not abdicate a single responsibility. He had left her in capable hands, well on the road to recovery. She came home to find he had arranged for someone to mow her yard, prune and weed her previously neglected flowerbeds, even air out her house that morning before she arrived. The guys at the station had taken her cat, let him live at the station and returned him to her house the day before she was released so he was there to greet her. There were vases of fresh wildflowers in every room, but no note.

She wasn't due at work for another couple of weeks and the inactivity only enhanced her frustration. Whether she read a novel, chose something on TV, or lay down for one of a multitude of naps, inevitably he was there in her mind.

Those serious eyes, those arousing hands. His voice. As her strength returned, so did her libido, and she touched herself in the desolate hours of the night and longed for her clever but mechanical fingers to be his. She almost called him a hundred times. When she put down the receiver for time one hundred and one, she figured it out.

Since Chicago, she'd been afraid to open her heart, give herself to a man. Justin had to force her to consider the possibility again because she'd been as terrified as the victim of a convenience store crime venturing out for a pack of cigarettes again. He'd given her a taste of what was possible.

More pain, certainly. Failure, very possibly. Or, if all the pieces fell in the right place, and they were both willing to devote themselves to making it work, a lifetime commitment. The love she'd been looking for in her first marriage. But if he was going to commit to it, he wanted her to do it too, out in the open. A straight-forward declaration, no hiding behind trumped up slights or imagined betrayals.

He thought he was so clever, presenting it like some noble sacrifice on his part, looking at her with those heated eyes, mouth curving in that way that made her remember just what those lips could do to her. While she was lying in her sickbed no less, where even imagining sex of such explosive proportions could kill her.

Well, she wasn't on her deathbed now, and she missed him, and he'd pissed her off again. He was going to answer for it. She decided to go to Fred's Pharmacy and get a double chocolate milkshake, complete with mini chocolate peanut butter cups. Then she'd call Linda.

Chapter 17

𝕤𝕠

Justin had avoided driving by Sarah's house as much as possible, but today there was no help for it. Linda and the coven were meeting him at a meadow off of Route 17. They were scoping it out as a perfect area for the first multi-county pagan festival they were planning to host and wanted his thoughts on it.

Her car wasn't there.

She was putting effort into avoiding him. Not one time in the past several weeks since she had gotten out of the hospital had he seen her, not even at a distance. Fine, then. If she didn't have the guts to reach out and take love when it was offered to her, he'd just…be miserable, go drag a commitment out of her, force her to accept him as he knew her heart and soul already did.

No, that's not the way it worked. If she'd made her choice, so be it. But he would damn well call her or maybe go see her if he didn't hear from her by the end of the week, so she would have to tell him to his face. He wouldn't press her, but he…oh hell, yes he would. He was in aching, screaming misery, his heart and his cock brothers-in-arms, tormenting him for the stupidity of his resolve. Wasn't all fair in love and war? Who was he to change the rules and give her a choice? He deserved this misery. Fools deserved what they got.

He checked his map and made the turn off the highway onto the rural route, hugging the edge of the road to get past the sawhorse barrier left by a road crew that Linda had warned him about. He absently noted it was very isolated and lovely, as she had promised. The road was little more than a dirt track after the first mile. He didn't see a farm or home, which suggested protected wetlands. If they could find a dry clearing for parking, this would be a good place.

He started at the sound of a siren and glanced up in his mirror.

"What the—"

There was a state trooper behind him. Great. The officer must have seen him going around the barrier and was investigating. He pulled over and shifted to get his wallet out of his back pocket.

"Sir, keep your hands on the wheel."

The megaphone was startling in the pastoral quiet. He immediately complied, his brow furrowed. The command took him by surprise, but he knew better than to argue with a cop before they got acquainted. An image of Sarah cuffed and writhing beneath him flashed through his brain, and he almost groaned at the longing that gripped him in a tight, painful vise.

The trooper's voice was a woman's, though distorted by the microphone. She pulled past him, turning the car in front of him at an angle.

The door opened and her legs came out, clad in the fawn-colored trousers tucked into polished black boots. She rose and her back was to him as she adjusted her gun belt and her hat. She bent back in to retrieve something.

While his thoughts and heart were firmly locked on Sarah, Justin Herne was a very sexual man, and one who noticed women. This female trooper was wearing the tightest pair of trooper jodhpurs he'd ever seen, stretched so taut over her skin it clearly defined the crack of that terrific ass, and the fact there was no way she was wearing underwear.

"What kind of officer—" and then she turned.

He blinked. She wore the short-sleeved thin summer-weight uniform shirt that went with the pale breeches, and she was all but spilling out of it. Her breasts were pushed together and displayed up high in a black lace shelf bra. He knew this, because the top two buttons of the undersized shirt were open so he could see the quivering top of her breasts, barely tucked into the cups. As she headed toward him, the effect was enhanced by the sway of her hips, exacerbated by the weight of the gun on her hip. Her hand rested lightly on it. It had taken him a full thirty seconds to reach her face. Moist pink lips and fiery blue eyes, her pale white-gold hair pulled up under the hat.

"Holy Mother—"

She stopped at the lowered window of the convertible BMW. "I think I told you to keep your hands on the wheel, Mr. Herne," she purred, bending over, her hand braced on the door. In that posture, with her hand still on her belt, he was staring into two perfectly displayed breasts within licking distance, if he had any saliva to use. Stupidly, he obeyed, returning his hands to the wheel. "Sarah, what—"

In a quick move he would have seen coming if his mind hadn't been so boggled with lust and shock, she pulled the handcuffs from the back of her belt and locked his right wrist to the base of the steering wheel.

However, the position required her to lean further over him. He recovered his wits enough to grab her neck with his free hand, knocking her hat off so her blonde ponytail spilled over her shoulder. He caught her mouth with his and plundered, not caring that she might be arresting him, just needing desperately to drink from that mouth he hadn't had in weeks and needed right now. Even if he died in the next moment, which was possible, since she was armed.

He wanted to fill his hands with those ripe breasts as well but was afraid to let go, afraid she'd pull back and he'd be forced to rip his steering wheel out of its column to get her.

She pulled back gasping, her lips swollen. She ducked out from under his hand and stepped back from the car. Justin shoved open the door and lunged after her. The cuff brought him up short, making him stand in the open doorway as she stayed a maddening foot out of reach.

She was getting her breath back, though he wished she wouldn't, for her erratic breathing did wonderful things with that shirt. He could tell for certain now she wasn't wearing underwear, for the trousers cut into her pussy, defining the labia for his gaze. Silently he begged to see that area darken with moisture, proving his effect on her.

Good Lord, Herne, get a grip. You're acting like a randy teenager.

"In this situation," she said, somehow managing to come across officious and stern, even with a hitch in her voice, "an officer typically tells you your rights. I'm going to tell you what rights you *don't* have anymore."

So here it was. An elaborate way to dump him and cruel, but he knew he had it coming. He wished she'd just take out the gun and shoot him, because that would be less painful.

"You see these?" She lifted her left hand, showing him a set of glossy nails, filed to smooth curves and painted a delicate pink that looked so attractive on her he wanted to suck each fingertip. "This is one of the many things I have done during my recuperation. A weekly manicure. One of the countless, inane, trivial things you do to keep yourself from going completely insane when you're out of death's door, but not quite up to your daily job. But I discovered something nice about these nails, Justin. Well-manicured nails feel very stimulating when you caress yourself."

Her fingers slid into the open collar of the shirt and stroked over the top of one rounded curve. He swallowed, but she wasn't done. Her fingertip straightened, slid down the deep cleft between them, then down over her stomach to the top of her thigh, so close to that well outlined pubic area he wished he had the magic to will her to touch herself.

"I did a lot of that, Justin. I'd lie there in my bed, alone, and I'd caress myself. I imagined my fingers were your tongue, your lips, the slide of your cock in my cunt. I'd be wet just thinking about it, even before I ran these glossy nails over my clit, gave it a light bite with them, the way I'd imagine your teeth would do it."

"I can do it now, if you'll just come here," he said impatiently.

"You left me there," she said, slicing through his words. "Left me with nurses and doctors, and my own thoughts."

"I thought you—"

"No." She held up that hand. "Number one. You don't have the right to speak until I'm through. So shut up, or I swear I'll pistol whip your testicles."

He winced. "Jesus, Sarah."

"Number two." Her fingers closed into a ball with two digits lifted. "You don't ever have the right to pull a stunt like you did in the hospital." Her eyes met his, and what he saw there stilled him, the deep flame of volcanic lava, simmering just on the edge of eruption. "Do you know that after I was shot, I was in the hospital about the same amount of time?"

Herne shook his head, because she raised a brow expectantly for an answer. "No, I didn't know that."

"Of course you didn't. It was pretty much like it was this time. You wander in this nebulous state of life and death, not sure which way you should go. It's clear which is which, you don't get confused about that. Life is harsh fluorescent lights, chemical smells, pain. Every time I surfaced, if I saw my husband, I saw the truth of our life together on his face. He was there, but he already wasn't there. I knew it. I had to choose life for myself, just for me, knowing he didn't want me anymore."

"Oh, Sarah." He reached out a hand for her, but she shook her head, stepped back.

"I'm not telling you this for your sympathy. This time, every time I surfaced, *you* were there. Not just waiting for me to get up so we could go back to having a relationship where we'd pretend we were devoted to each other. Not just there because you had a week's worth of lust and attraction for me boiling through your system."

She took a deep breath, and it shuddered through her. Justin realized in sudden anguish that she was fighting tears. If they spilled from those blue eyes, he had no doubt he'd go to his knees and beg for the right to touch her.

"No, you were *there*, by my side, in my head, in my heart. This time I knew I'd make it *because* you were there, not in spite of that. Do you know how terrifying it was to realize my heart was that dependent on you after less than a week of knowing you? So, Number Three. This is the big one, Herne, so pay attention." She blinked twice, swallowed, pointed one of those glossy nails at him.

"You don't have the right to play games with me, to make me choose you. To make me lower my shields when it's already so blessed obvious how important you are to me. I can't handle that." Her voice caught, and she averted her face from him.

"Sarah." He moved forward, and the cuff caught him again. "Damn it," he exploded. "Come here and take this off, or I swear I'll rip the damn steering wheel out."

She was crying without making a sound, her shoulders shaking.

"For God's sake, let me hold you. I've wanted to do nothing else since I left your side. Do you know every time I heard a car come down the road I practically mowed down my customers to look out the window? I got a damn crick in my neck."

"You could have come to me."

"No, Sarah," he said. "I'm sorry, so sorry. My intention wasn't to play games with you, I swear. I wanted you to be sure when you chose, because I was already certain about you. I knew the first time we made love in your house, but even if I hadn't been certain then, I was the night...that night when we stopped him."

She turned her head to look at him. He didn't want to bring it up, knew it haunted her, but she could handle hearing about it, he knew it. Nothing defeated her. He wondered at what he had done to earn the blessing of her in his life.

"Everything was laid bare, Sarah. You knew it, felt it, just as I did. In that moment, with the Lord and Lady in us, our souls knew that we were meant for each other. I love you, Sarah. It was there, just waiting, since that first second I saw you. Our minds haven't caught up to it, but it's in my heart and soul and I wanted you to choose. I wouldn't take half, or stand the wait."

She stared at him, defiant still, her eyes bright with new tears.

"I'm begging you, Sarah," he rasped. "Let me hold you. I've been hard as a rock for days, and all I've wanted is you."

"All right," she murmured, and he thought they were the most sacred two words he'd ever heard.

She came toward him. One step, two steps, and she was there. Before she could reach for the key, he had his free arm around her, crushing her to him, holding her with her face against his neck. Her arms came up to twine around his back and waist and she trembled in his embrace.

"I thought I had lost you," he said into her hair, and he meant the night of the incubus as much as when he had to walk out on her at the hospital.

"Never," she said, muffled against his skin. She tilted her head. He kissed the salt of her tears away, tasted her with his tongue. She made a sound in the back of her throat and pressed her body against him. He insinuated his thigh between her legs and she opened for him there, whimpering in that maddening way when she rubbed against him.

"You put on some weight since I last saw you," he said, his hand palming one cheek of her bottom and clamping down hard, savoring the feel of her squirming, her quick smile.

"I've been drinking milkshakes everyday," she informed him. "Doctor's orders."

"Anything else gotten rounder and fatter?"

"Your lip, if you keep it up, Herne."

He grinned. "You going to let me go?"

She leaned past him, biting her lip as his free hand slid around to cup her crotch and found her blessedly wet. Her eyes twinkled, a mixture of lust and joy, and quick as she unsnapped the cuff from the wheel, she clapped it down on that other errant wrist, locking his hands together.

"Sarah, what the—"

She snaked her arms through the locked ring of his and closed her fingers over his ass. "Improvise."

He slanted her a glance. Arrogance and raging hunger changed to calculation so quickly she barely had time to blink. "Hold on," he warned her.

He stepped back so her arms slid free and then brought his hands up and over her, so she was bound in the circle of his arms against him. He caught her buttocks in his hands and tightened his grip to alert her before he used his strength to hitch her up on his body. Sarah obliged with an accommodating hop and wrapped her legs around his waist, gasping at the feel of his erection pressed against the base of her soaked pussy.

He turned, took them around the door, slamming it with his knee, and laid her back on the hood of the car. He tried to be careful, but his need made it a rougher descent than expected. She didn't mind.

Though he was restrained, he very quickly made it obvious she had become his captive. His cuffed hands, behind her back, slid down her ass and beneath her thighs, those clever fingers finding the seam of the tight trousers.

"Justin," she gasped. He ripped them with a sheer brutal male strength that delighted her and made her tremble at once.

"Yes." She arched against him, rubbing her now bare cunt against the turgid arousal under his trousers. As she arched, one of the buttons of the small shirt popped loose and rolled, and her breasts spilled out before his hot eyes. The areola and nipple of her left breast had worked free of the bra cup and was now visible over the edge of the lace. He leaned down, grinding his cock hard against her. He latched onto the nipple, the tatting and his tongue rubbing rough and soft against her at once.

There was no warning. All the alarms went off in her body and she managed just a whisper of air before she came, just from that pressure and the sucking of his lips. She cried out his name. He kept up the suckling, the rubbing of his hips against her as she bucked. The metal of the cuffs bit into her skin as her back bowed and her shoulder blades thumped against the warm surface of the car, her body convulsing with the force of the climax.

Even as she vibrated with aftershocks, he would not let her rest. "Open my trousers, Sarah," he ordered, biting her throat. "I need to fuck you."

Her fingers trembled and she could barely manage the belt, but she did, taking down his zipper and his underwear. He let her get the garment to his thighs, but before she could close her hands around his pulsing, thick length, those capable hands shifted and twisted her. With a squeak she was in the air and flipped over, her thighs pressed against the grill, knees on the bumper, her booted toes off the ground. He sheathed himself deep in her cunt in one fluid movement, sinking himself to the hilt against her, along tissues so exquisitely sensitive from her orgasm that she screamed, part pleasure, part pain, but accepting all of it, all of him.

The weight of his chest was on her back and he set his teeth back to her throat, all male animal now, all rutting stag, claiming his mate in the oldest way known to all beasts.

"Mine," he murmured, underscoring her thoughts, recalling the other times he had said it to her, though this was the first time she believed it, embraced its truth.

The few times they had been together had been explosive, but he had always shown some level of control or artistic finesse, and her body and mind had deeply appreciated his skill at driving her body to peak. However, her primeval soul wanted only this now. He was not concerned with her climax as he drove into her hard, ruthlessly. He was sating his own need, lust and possession at once. Just the psychological impact of that ripped her over the next edge of control, and she would have bitten her fist, if it had not been held to her side. The binding on his arms locked hers against her, the metal of his handcuffed hands biting into her lower belly as his fingers dug into her hipbones and pelvis, holding her for his branding strokes.

She screamed again, her hips lifting to take him. He answered with a sound somewhere between a snarl and a guttural cry and his body thrust against hers, spilling his seed into her. She opened her legs wider, unspoken acceptance of him, and felt the heat of the car hood burn through her shirt and bra, warm her nipples just like his body sliding against her back, his thighs slapping her hips. She was all heat, liquid heat that boiled over and turned the world around her a swirling red and orange, mixing with the green of the fields.

When he collapsed upon her, and at last his heart slowed with hers, he showed tenderness and mercy. He turned his head, brushed his lips against her shoulder blade, her nape.

"I love you, Sarah," he said quietly.

She quivered beneath him, her eyes filling even as her lips curved in a smile. She pressed her cheek to warm metal and managed to look up at him with a sidelong glance. "God help us both. If it's always like this, we'll kill each other."

He chuckled and raised his upper body with a grunt of effort. He took her with him, bringing her attention to his bound wrists by cupping her breasts in his palms. The chain

197

rubbed the underside of the curves while his thumb played in the deep crease between them, sliding under the band of the bra.

"This looks like something from my shop, Chief Wylde. Have you moved on to breaking and entering?"

"Worse. I resorted to a lingerie competitor." Her head rested on his shoulder, her body still vibrating in his arms. "I hope you're appreciative. This thing is a torture device from the Inquisition."

"I'll be happy to soothe every red line away with my tongue." He nuzzled her neck, and continued to stroke his finger between the two breasts. "Slow licks to take the pain away."

She swallowed. "You are going to kill me," she said, and his eyes promised the delightful danger of it. "Why don't I release your hands?"

"I don't know. I'm learning just how enjoyable playing with handcuffs can be." His hands slid down from her breasts and played in her curls, the wet swollen lips of her pussy. Her breath left her and her head fell back on his shoulder again.

"You were supposed to be my prisoner."

"I like how this worked out." He smiled.

"I admit I've never looked at them quite the way you do. They're typically a serve-and-protect type of thing. You know, criminal element and all."

"I know." His hands stilled, went to her waist and convinced her to turn in that protective circle to face him. His mouth was sober all of a sudden, his eyes hard. "It's going to be difficult for me, Sarah. I want to protect you, love you, but you do a job that doesn't let me protect you much. It's not in your nature to stay in Lilesville forever. You'll eventually want to go back to where your talents are needed even more."

"It's hard for a lot of cops' lovers, particularly men," she admitted, some trepidation rising in her. "I guess...you'll have to think it over some..."

"No." He shook his head, squeezed her ass in reprimand. "That's not what I mean, Sarah. What do I have to offer *you*? I can't protect you from the things you see in your job."

"Oh." It had never occurred to her, that someone might think about it that way. A warmth spread out of a place deep inside her, dispelling the cold fear she had carried around for so long. The heat reached her gaze as she raised her lashes and stared into his eyes.

"No, you can't," she said softly. "But you can protect me from my nightmares. I can handle my own reality, if you can handle that. You saved me from this one."

He studied her a long moment, then nodded. "I can do that."

He went to one knee and rested the side of his face against her abdomen just below her breasts. It was a gesture of comfort, an offer and a request all at once. Sarah laid her hands on his head, bent her own to it and laid a kiss there, feeling his soft hair tickle her mouth, the press of his hands against her hips. They stayed that way some time, letting the soft wind be the only sound, loosening and freeing the pain of the past few weeks, leaving them clean.

"So." He lifted his head at last and gave her a thorough perusal. "I'd say you pulled in some heavy favors for this one."

"Pretty heavy," she agreed.

"Remind me to give her generous gift certificates."

"You better. You just tore the hell out of her uniform." She gazed ruefully down at the frayed shirt and trousers. "And I helped."

"Good Lord, she must be a pixie."

"Weighs a hundred pounds sopping wet, and is meaner than any trooper three times her size, so it better be a really good gift certificate, if you value your lover's skin."

"I do, very much." He placed his lips on it and she closed her eyes, hummed a sigh. "Very well, then. A lifetime supply of hopping penises."

"You—"

He laughed at her and ducked her swat. Sarah fished her key off her belt and Justin reluctantly stood, lifting his arms from over her head. He brought them down before her so she could unlock the restraints.

When the cuff dropped from his left wrist, he startled her by lifting her and thrusting his cock into her. He was half hard for her again already, and her pussy was slippery enough to take him.

He buried himself in her, there was no other word for it. A thrust into a wet passage eager just for him, the summation of everything that ever was. A release from prison, a meal of homemade bread and gurgling cold water for a person stranded in the desert, the miracle of life being handed back when only death was expected. The simple joy of a hand reached for and there to be held, forever.

She gasped and he eased her back on the hood, leaning over her, very close, studying her face. That quiet moment of stillness she remembered from their first night descended, and this time she embraced it. She reached up, touched his face, framed it with her hands, brought him down to her for that tender kiss.

"I figured out the most important treatment for healing wounds," she murmured.

"Did you? What was it, darling?"

She smiled at the endearment, drew in another trembling breath as he rubbed himself inside her, slow circling strokes.

"I used to believe we have to heal our own wounds to be able to love others, but I don't think that's true. All we need to do is accept the love of others, because there are broken places that can't be healed without that. It would be like a pitcher trying to glue its own handle back on."

She looked into those dark eyes, so intent on hers. Her truth was there in them.

"I love you, Justin. Take me home."

Why an electronic book?

We live in the Information Age—an exciting time in the history of human civilization, in which technology rules supreme and continues to progress in leaps and bounds every minute of every day. For a multitude of reasons, more and more avid literary fans are opting to purchase e-books instead of paper books. The question from those not yet initiated into the world of electronic reading is simply: *Why?*

1. *Price.* An electronic title at Ellora's Cave Publishing and Cerridwen Press runs anywhere from 40% to 75% less than the cover price of the exact same title in paperback format. Why? Basic mathematics and cost. It is less expensive to publish an e-book (no paper and printing, no warehousing and shipping) than it is to publish a paperback, so the savings are passed along to the consumer.

2. *Space.* Running out of room in your house for your books? That is one worry you will never have with electronic books. For a low one-time cost, you can purchase a handheld device specifically designed for e-reading. Many e-readers have large, convenient screens for viewing. Better yet, hundreds of titles can be stored within your new library—on a single microchip. There are a variety of e-readers from different manufacturers. You can also read e-books on your PC or laptop computer. (Please note that Ellora's Cave does not endorse any specific brands.

You can check our websites at www.ellorascave.com or www.cerridwenpress.com for information we make available to new consumers.)

3. *Mobility.* Because your new e-library consists of only a microchip within a small, easily transportable e-reader, your entire cache of books can be taken with you wherever you go.

4. *Personal Viewing Preferences.* Are the words you are currently reading too small? Too large? Too… ANNOYING? Paperback books cannot be modified according to personal preferences, but e-books can.

5. *Instant Gratification.* Is it the middle of the night and all the bookstores near you are closed? Are you tired of waiting days, sometimes weeks, for bookstores to ship the novels you bought? Ellora's Cave Publishing sells instantaneous downloads twenty-four hours a day, seven days a week, every day of the year. Our webstore is never closed. Our e-book delivery system is 100% automated, meaning your order is filled as soon as you pay for it.

Those are a few of the top reasons why electronic books are replacing paperbacks for many avid readers.

As always, Ellora's Cave and Cerridwen Press welcome your questions and comments. We invite you to email us at Comments@ellorascave.com or write to us directly at Ellora's Cave Publishing Inc., 1056 Home Avenue, Akron, OH 44310-3502.